MY SON, BELOVED STRANGER

Can Kate accept her gay son?
Can her church?

KATE McLAUGHLIN

Pacific Press Publishing Association
Boise, Idaho
Oshawa, Ontario, Canada

Edited by Kenneth R. Wade
Designed by Tim Larson
Cover illustration by Dynamic Graphics©
Typeset in Bookman 10/12

Library of Congress Cataloging-in-Publication Data:

McLaughlin, Kate, 1936-
     My Son, Beloved Stranger / Kate McLaughlin.
        p. cm.
     ISBN 0-8163-1257-5
     I. Title
    PS3563.C38377B4 1995
    813'.54—dc20   95-3295
                                          CIP

95 96 97 98 99 • 5 4 3 2 1

Contents

1. Broken Engagement 7
2. Thinking the Unthinkable 17
3. What Is a Homosexual? 26
4. Spring Break 34
5. How Will I Tell Michael? 42
6. Is Danny Going to Be Lost? 51
7. A Heartache Shared 65
8. It's Not Fair! 76
9. Prejudice 84
10. Christmas 90
11. Steve 96
12. AIDS Conference 105
13. Graduation 114
14. Ups and Downs: Letters From Danny 121
15. Bittersweet Wedding 127
16. Michael 130
17. Danny's Decision 139

Dedicated
to Danny

Because of you, we have a clearer understanding
of God's everlasting love for each of us,
His broken, sin-scarred children.

Acknowledgments

Without the encouragement, prodding, suggestions,
and advice of the following people,
this book might never have been written:
Danny, Nancy Irland, Fern Babcock,
Dorothy Watts, Miriam Wood, and members of
the Western Washington Adventist Writers Association,
especially Maylan Schurch and Marian Forschler.

Explanation

Names and events have been altered
to protect the privacy of some individuals.

Chapter 1

Broken Engagement

Huge snowflakes drifted softly down from the pewter-colored sky, outlining each individual branch and twig in the woods and piling up on the ground. Inside, logs burned in the fireplace, crackling a cozy counterpoint to the Brahms symphony on the stereo. The delectable aroma of baking bread and simmering soup wafted from the kitchen.

On this late-winter afternoon, Kate sat by the window quilting. She looked with satisfaction at the squares of coral and indigo blue, entwined in an Irish Chain pattern that outlined crisp squares of white in which she was quilting a hearts-and-flowers pattern. It was to be a wedding gift for her youngest son and his bride-to-be.

Kate sighed contentedly. *Could anything be more perfect?* she mused. Glancing out the window, her busy needle paused as her eye caught the scarlet flash of a cardinal flying across the snowy yard. *Yes*, she thought with a smile, *God always has something more.*

The front door opened, and Michael, Kate's husband of thirty-two years, blew in with a blast of cold air, disturbing her reverie. "Six weeks in South America should be quite a change from this weather!" he exclaimed, stomping the snow from his feet.

Kate smiled. "Don't rub it in! You've got ten more days of this stuff."

"And then, sunny Argentina!" Michael found room for his jacket in the closet.

"Well, I suppose Argentina will be nice," Kate admitted, "but how about hot, sticky Brazil? And besides, you'll miss seeing Danny."

Michael dropped into his favorite chair by the fireplace. "Yeah, I wish I were going to be back in time for spring break." He sighed. "Seems like I've had to be away so many times when the kids were home."

Watching him, Kate's eyes lingered lovingly on his face and the dusting of gray at his temples. It didn't seem possible they had been married for so long. But here they were, grandparents, and Danny, their youngest, was busy with wedding plans.

Michael looked at his watch. "I'm surprised Danny hasn't called yet. He always calls on Sunday."

"I'm anxious to hear about their wedding invitations," Kate responded. "I think he and Angela were supposed to decide on them this week." As if on cue, the phone rang. Kate grinned and raced Michael to answer it. She won, and Michael went to pick up the extension in the study.

"Hi, Danny!" Kate said warmly. "We were just talking about you and wondering when you'd call. How's everything going?"

"Well, I got an A on my paper for Children's Lit. I think Dr. Johnson likes *Harriet, the Spy* as much as I do!" laughed Danny. "I still have two more papers to finish before break, but I think I'll make it. Did I tell you I'm going to be the 'good' thief on the cross for the passion play?"

"No, you hadn't told us," Kate said. "If only you weren't clear across the country! I would love to be there to see it. . . . Well . . . , I'm dying to know. Did you and Angela get down to San Jose to pick out your invitations?"

There was an awkward pause. Then, hesitantly, Danny said, "Uh, Mom . . . , Dad . . . , I don't know exactly how to tell you this, but, uh . . . , Angie and I have decided to postpone our wedding."

Kate was stunned! For a moment, she felt as if ice water were coursing through her veins. "But why?" she finally managed. "What's happened? Have you had a fight?"

"Oh no," Danny answered, a bit uncomfortably. "It's just that we have such different philosophies of life. We need some time to work things out."

Questions raced through Kate's mind. What did he mean, "different philosophies"?

"You and Angie haven't broken things off completely, have you?" Michael asked. "She's such a sweet girl, Danny. Mom and I really like her a lot."

"Oh, we're still good friends, Dad," Danny said quickly. "I'm sorry to make you feel bad, but I thought I should let you know." He sounded anxious and troubled.

"It's OK, honey." Kate tried to be reassuring. "It's just such a surprise . . . After you've been engaged for over two years, it seems like you would have known before this if you didn't share the same outlook on life . . . But I know this isn't easy for you. We'll be praying for you, honey, and I hope everything will work out."

"Thanks, Mom." Danny changed the conversation to a more comfortable topic. "Aren't you leaving on a trip pretty soon, Dad?"

They talked about Michael's upcoming trip to South America as part of his responsibilities as a church administrator. Kate wanted to know more about Danny and Angela, but she forced herself not to ask any questions. Danny would tell her when he was ready, she was sure of that. They had always had a very close relationship.

At last they said goodbye. As Kate hung up the phone and stared out the window, a sense of foreboding wrapped chill fingers around her heart. Her intuition told her something was terribly wrong, something she couldn't quite grasp.

"I just don't understand it!" Michael exclaimed, coming into the room. "They never seemed to have any problems that I could see."

"I know," answered Kate with a puzzled frown. "Angela seems to fit so well into our family."

In another phone call from Danny a few days later, it became clear that the wedding was really off, not just postponed. Surprisingly, Danny seemed more relieved than disappointed. To say that Kate and Michael were disappointed was to put it mildly. They had become very fond of Angela over the past two years.

"I wonder whose idea this was. He'll never find another girl like Angie!" declared Michael. "I still can't understand what went wrong."

"She was just the kind of girl I always dreamed of for a daughter-in-law," said Kate wistfully. "Remember how she loved to help me cook last summer? And how she got out and washed the car with you on Fridays? She has a lot of good common sense, just what Danny needs to balance his idealistic views. What in the world did he mean about them having different philosophies of life?"

But Michael couldn't figure it out either.

As Kate was folding shirts and putting them in the suitcase the evening before Michael was to leave for South America, she thought about how lonely the drive to the office would be when he was gone. *However*, she reminded herself, *by the time he gets back, I'll be used to it and be enjoying my opportunity for solitude. The adjustment never gets any easier when you have a husband who travels*, she thought with a sigh.

The phone rang, interrupting her musing. It was Angela's mother.

"Oh, I'm just so disappointed!" moaned Martha. "I've been crying all week since Angela told me. What's wrong with these kids, anyway? It doesn't make any sense to me. Did Danny tell you why they broke up?"

"Just something about them having different philosophies of life, but I don't know what in the world he meant. I was going to call you myself, since you're there on the West Coast with them. Did you have any idea this was going to happen?"

"No, it was a complete shock to me. I was surprised when they didn't come down to pick out their invitations, but I never dreamed they were having any problems."

Martha's voice trembled. "I love Danny like he was my own child. I keep hoping this is just a 'lover's quarrel' and they'll patch things up and get back together soon. Don't you?"

Tears sprang to Kate's eyes. "Nothing would make me happier," she said softly. "If only we knew what had happened."

"The next time Angela comes home, I'm going to get to the bottom of this!" exclaimed Martha. "If I knew why they made this crazy decision, I'd know how to talk some sense into them."

"Well, we'd better be careful not to push them too much," cautioned Kate. "Let's pray about it. Maybe God will help them remember what a wonderful relationship they have had."

"You're right, and I have been praying about it a lot already," Martha said. "Let's keep in touch, Kate. Let me know if you find out what the problem is."

A few days later, still troubled about Danny, Kate cradled a steaming cup of hot chocolate in both hands as she stood in front of the kitchen sink and gazed out the window at the swirling white flakes of another spring snowstorm.

Snow . . . Her mind drifted back to a long-ago Christmas season in Singapore. They had been new missionaries, recently arrived from Hawaii.

Nearly forty missionary families lived on two compounds in the large cosmopolitan city. They administered the work of the church in fourteen Asian countries, as well as a local hospital and college. A small yellow bus transported the school-age children living on Kate and Michael's compound to the school for missionary children, located on the other compound.

"Here come the brothers," called three-year-old Danny one afternoon, watching from the window as the returning schoolchildren streamed up the hill under big black umbrellas. Brenden and Alex burst noisily into the house.

"Hey, Mom, we put up the Christmas tree at school today," reported Brenden, who was ten. "Why don't we get out *our* new tree and put it up?"

Kate looked at the gray sky and the rain streaming down the window in a tropical downpour. "As long as I'm inside with the air conditioner on, I can almost believe it's winter," she laughed. "Too bad Daddy won't be back for another week. Do you think we could figure out how to put it together by ourselves?"

"Of course we can," said Alex, with all the authority of a seventh-grader. "I'll get the box out of the storeroom."

"OK," Kate gave her assent. "While you're getting it, I'll find our Christmas records and the ornaments. We might as well really get in the mood!"

Soon the living room was heaped with piles of dark green imitation Scotch pine branches of various lengths. Kate looked dubiously at the long wooden pole drilled full of holes. "I don't think this is going to look very much like a real tree."

"Look! Here's a little Christmas tree!" sang Danny, picking out a small cluster of branches and dancing around the room.

"That goes on the top." Brenden snatched it from him and stood on tiptoe to push it down into the hole on the end of the pole.

Alex was studying the instruction sheet. "Put the branches with the white tip on the wire into the top row of holes," he commanded. His three slaves quickly obeyed. When all the branches were finally placed, Kate had to admit that it was a beautiful tree, indeed, except for its missing ingredient— the fresh, evocative, piney scent of outdoors.

Three strings of miniature lights were carefully wound around the tree from top to bottom. Danny hung little red rocking horses, his favorite ornaments, on the lower branches, while Brenden and Alex competed to see who could hang the most crocheted snowflakes. Kate tucked gold filigreed stars into the bare spots.

Then with her three boys lined up on the couch and the lights turned off, Kate announced, "Now comes the magic moment!"

The sweet, clear soprano voices of the Vienna Choir Boys singing "Away in a Manger" set the mood as Kate plugged in the lights. She caught her breath at the unguarded look of wonder in three pairs of eyes reflecting the soft rainbow glow. They admired the tree in silent contentment.

"Mom, I know what you should read Danny for his bedtime story tonight," Brenden said. He went into his bedroom and returned with a well-worn blue book, which he thrust into her lap.

" 'Twas the night before Christmas . . ." read Kate with a smile. Danny snuggled up on one side and Brenden sat down on the other. Even Alex stayed by, listening reflectively to the familiar poem.

"Mommy, when is it going to snow?" Danny asked when she had finished.

"Oh, honey, I'm afraid it won't snow here. It didn't snow in Hawaii, remember?" Kate reminded him.

"I know it didn't snow in Hawaii, but I think it will snow in Singapore," Danny said, nodding his head with the utmost confidence. His bedtime prayer included a request for snow before Christmas. Kate suppressed a smile as she tucked him into bed and kissed him good night.

"Poor kid," Alex said when she told him about it, "he's never seen snow in his life. He doesn't know what he's missing." Alex spoke condescendingly from his much wider life experience, which included an unusual six-inch snowfall in California's high desert during his seventh winter.

The next afternoon, Kate was in the kitchen rolling out piecrusts when she heard shouts and giggles coming from the living room. She looked in to see Danny lying on the floor, looking up in blissful delight at a swirling white blizzard.

"We wanted to show Danny what snow is like," explained Brenden. He and Alex had torn several sheets of paper into tiny bits, heaped them onto the blades of the ceiling fan, and turned it on slow speed to create a realistic snowstorm.

"Do it again!" shouted Danny, jumping up and starting to gather up "snowflakes" from all over the living room.

Kate's lips curved in a smile as she looked at the snow swirling past her window and remembered the fake snowstorm of long ago. Her cocoa had cooled. As she reheated it, she remembered that Danny's disappointment over the lack of snow had been assuaged by the fun of dressing up in the

Nativity costumes she had made for her children's class at church. Michael had taken pictures of Danny dressed as a wise man, a shepherd, and Joseph, but his favorite costume was Mary's deep blue gown and azure headscarf. He had made an especially charming Mary, looking tenderly down at the baby in his arms. How he had loved playing dress-up as a little boy. The two little Indian girls he played with had even given him one of their outgrown saris, she remembered.

Kate carried her cocoa into the family room and turned on the TV, flipping idly through the channels until she reached the public television station. To her surprise, it was a live performance by Moscow's famed Bolshoi Ballet. The familiar strains of Tchaikovsky's *Swan Lake* carried her thoughts back again to their first furlough, three years after their arrival in Singapore.

They had all spent many hours in planning the long-anticipated trip. After much discussion, they decided to purchase their air tickets through Aeroflot, the Russian airline, which had the lowest prices. This would give them the opportunity to spend a couple of days in Moscow before flying on to Vienna, London, and the States.

"Oh, I hope we can see a ballet performance by the Bolshoi!" exclaimed Kate. Alex and Brenden groaned.

When they toured the Kremlin, Kate was excited to learn that the Bolshoi was performing *Swan Lake* that very evening. Later, in the darkened concert hall, she looked over at her youngest son, kneeling on the red velvet seat beside her. While Alex and Brenden yawned in boredom, Danny gripped the armrests and peered between rows of heads at the brilliant stage, staring in rapt fascination as the dancers swirled and pirouetted, one with the music that tiptoed and soared around him. His eyes were shining, his lips parted in a faint smile, and he almost forgot to breathe, he was so enchanted by the magical beauty. The graceful white figures, gliding like swans, seemed brought to life by the music that swelled and burst inside of him.

Then the ballet was over, and crashing applause exploded around them. The house lights came up, accompanied by a buzz of conversation, and Danny filed out after the rest of the family, still lost in a world of wonder and delight. As they reached the street, Danny tugged excitedly at Kate's hand.

"Mommy, I want to be a ballerina when I grow up!"

Alex and Brenden laughed. "Only girls can be ballerinas, silly!" Brenden told him.

Danny looked anxiously at Kate for confirmation.

"Men can be ballet dancers too," she assured him. "Like the prince in *Swan Lake.*"

"But I want to be a ballerina and wear a skirt that stands out like this when I twirl around," insisted Danny, holding his arms out straight at his sides and executing a pirouette.

Kate had forgotten the incident by the time they returned to their mission home at the end of the summer, but Danny had not. "Remember the ballerinas we saw in Moscow, Mommy? Will you make me a skirt like that, *please*?"

Kate was scarcely aware of a faint but familiar tightness as she quickly shoved an uneasy feeling deep down into her subconscious. "Oh, you don't want to wear a skirt, honey," she laughed.

"Yes, I do," insisted Danny earnestly. "I want to be a swan and twirl around on one toe like the ballerinas."

Over the next few days, Danny kept up a persistent campaign to get a skirt until at last, with a sigh, Kate looked through her fabric collection and pulled out a narrow length of material, stitched the ends together, made a hem on one edge and a casing on the other, and threaded elastic through the casing.

"There's your ballerina skirt," she said, handing it to him.

"Thanks, Mom!" Danny exclaimed happily, pulling it on and spinning away from her.

Well, he's still just a little boy, she thought ruefully. *He'll soon outgrow such ideas.*

And he did, Kate remembered, after he started school.

She had been awakened early one morning by a small hand insistently patting her shoulder. Sleepily, she opened her eyes.

"It's time to get up, Mom! I've already made my bed!" Danny informed her.

"Oh, Danny!" Kate murmured with a grin. "It's the first day of school, isn't it? Well, I guess we'd better get around. You sure wouldn't want to miss the school bus!"

Danny was almost too excited to eat, and when the bus driver tooted his horn, he flew eagerly to the door. Kate caught a kiss as he sped by.

As the weeks passed, however, Kate noticed that Danny's enthusiasm for school seemed to be waning, and some days he appeared quite dejected. One afternoon she stopped by the school to ask his teacher, Miss Summers, if she knew what was wrong.

"I'm afraid the big boys in third and fourth grade have been teasing him," Miss Summers apologized. "They're so much bigger than Danny, and they always want to play soccer at recess. Danny doesn't like such rough games and prefers to play with the girls. But sometimes the girls want to play by themselves, and then he is left out. I heard the boys calling him a sissy the other day, and I've talked to them about it. I'm watching to see that they don't tease him anymore."

Poor Danny, Kate thought sympathetically. *It's too bad there isn't another boy his age.*

At least, she realized, *he seems to have lost interest in dressing up.* She wondered if that had anything to do with the older boys teasing him.

Several days later, Alex, a protective big brother, reported disgustedly that he had heard some of the fourth-grade boys calling Danny a sissy. "I banged their heads together and told them to leave him alone!" he said heatedly.

Now Danny is in college, fighting his own battles, Kate mused. The ballet performance on TV was over, and she realized she had scarcely seen it, so absorbed had she been in the train of memories it had launched.

She took her empty cup to the kitchen, rinsed it out, and went to bed, disturbing thoughts running through her mind. Why do I feel so uneasy? she wondered as she drifted into a troubled sleep.

Chapter 2

Thinking the Unthinkable

Michael had been gone for a week, but it was Danny Kate couldn't stop thinking about. Unanswered questions about his broken engagement alternated with memories of his childhood.

A "surprise" baby, Danny had been born ten months after Kate and Michael arrived in Hawaii. They had hoped their third child would be a daughter. While she was pregnant, Kate had even made a tiny pair of pink overalls, trimmed in lace. But there was no disappointment or regret each time they looked into the bassinet and saw Danny's big brown eyes studying a fist or lighting up with interest as the faces of his brothers came into view.

Six-year-old Brenden was so eager to see his new brother that Michael had let him skip school the day he brought Kate and Danny home from the hospital. And even though Alex, at nine, was too grown up to admit his excitement, he headed straight for the bassinet the minute he got home from school.

As the months went by, Danny came to look forward to the after-school reunions with his brothers as much as they did. Before long, it became apparent that it was going to take some doing to keep up with Danny. At first, the boys thought it was fun teaching him to crawl, but they soon thought better of it. He took advantage of his new mobility to get into everything within reach, including their personal possessions.

As a toddler, Danny's zest for life had led him from one

17

escapade to another, Kate remembered with a grin. Like the time he had retrieved an egg from the unguarded refrigerator door and cracked it on the arm of a living-room chair. Or the time he had put her plastic hairbrush in the oven to bake. She had discovered that when a terrible smell filled the kitchen the next time she turned the oven on. And then there was the time he liberally salted the living-room carpet while his baby-sitting brothers were engrossed in a game. But he was so cute and lovable that his mischief usually resulted in laughter rather than exasperation.

And now, he's a handsome college junior who has just broken his engagement to a lovely young woman, Kate thought, with a sigh. *What could have happened?* She was still puzzling over the mystery as she wandered into the living room and picked up the latest issue of *National Geographic.* Carrying it to Michael's chair by the fireplace, she sat down and began leafing through the pages.

Suddenly, a chill tingled up her spine. She had turned to an article on Inverness, Scotland. The name triggered a deeply suppressed memory. She was transported back to a spring afternoon three years earlier.

She and Michael had just returned permanently to the United States after fifteen years in Singapore and were visiting Michael's mother in northern California. Nonnie, as they affectionately called her, had provided a "home away from home" for Alex and Brenden when they had returned to the States to attend college nearby.

On a pleasantly warm afternoon, they sat in green wooden lawn chairs under the ancient apple tree in the backyard. As Kate looked up into its gnarled branches, she remembered how her boys, one after the other, had learned to climb it and how they loved to eat the delicious applesauce Nonnie made from its fruit. She breathed in the cedar-scented air delightedly. How different this warmth was from the fierce heat of the tropics!

They missed PaPa, Michael's father. He had died of a heart attack five years earlier. Alex was there with his adorable little daughter Amy, but a fresh sense of loss smote Kate's heart as she looked at him. Aileen, the beautiful Japanese girl he had married after dropping out of college, had left him, and he was struggling to raise Amy alone and finish his degree. Kate could still vividly remember the sick feeling she had had in the pit of her stomach when Alex had told them about his impending divorce.

Brenden would fly home in one more week after his first year of teaching missionaries' children in Okinawa. And Danny, who had just graduated from twelfth grade at the mission school in Singapore, was enjoying a solo jaunt through England and Scotland to celebrate.

Michael was entertaining them all with exciting stories about his travels throughout the exotic countries of Asia. Kate smiled in amusement at Nonnie's obvious pride. She understood. She felt the same pride in her boys' achievements. And she was proud of Michael, too, glad that he really enjoyed his ministry and was good at it.

Nonnie disappeared into the house and soon came back out, carrying a tray with glasses; a big, frosty pitcher of lemonade; and a plate of chocolate-chip cookies. Setting it on the table, she proceeded to serve everyone, the ice cubes hitting the sides of the pitcher like melodious wind chimes.

"Nonnie, I think your goal in life is to make sure no one ever has an empty stomach," Kate said, laughing.

Amy reached eagerly for a cookie, then turned around to see if her daddy approved. He smiled and nodded. "Just one, OK?"

Michael took a big sip of lemonade. "M-m-m!" he said, appreciatively. "This is fresh squeezed, isn't it?"

Nonnie nodded.

"Kind of makes me lonesome for Danny," Kate said with a faraway look in her eyes. "He loves to bake chocolate-chip cookies, and he's always making us fresh lemonade."

"I wish Danny were here now, instead of traipsing around Europe all by himself," Nonnie said, with a worried frown.

"He'll be fine," Michael reassured her. "He originally planned to make this trip with a friend, but at the last minute, Max backed out, so he decided to go alone. It's really quite safe.

Lots of kids do it these days, you know." Michael drained his glass.

"Missionary kids are used to traveling, Nonnie," Alex added. "We're pretty capable and independent."

"Well, I still can't help worrying about him," insisted Nonnie. She fidgeted with her hands, then found something for them to do. "How about some more lemonade?" She held the pitcher poised expectantly.

"Sure," Michael said, holding out his glass. "You're just like Kate, you know. You should have heard her before Danny left." He mimicked Kate's voice. " 'Do be careful!' 'Be sure not to lose your plane ticket!' 'Keep your passport with you all the time!' 'Remember to keep track of your travelers' checks!' And 'Never lay your backpack down!' Honestly, you'd think she thought he was eight years old instead of eighteen."

Kate grinned wryly. She remembered how Danny had given her a quick hug, laughed, and said, "Relax, Mom! I'm a big boy now!"

"Well, I know how she feels," defended Nonnie. "A mother always keeps a little corner of her mind on alert when her child's away. I know I worried about you while you were overseas. All those plane trips and traveling in foreign countries."

Alex brought the conversation back to the present. "I suppose Danny took his camera," he speculated. Photography was among Danny's multitude of interests.

"Oh yes." Kate laughed as she pictured Danny shouldering his well-stuffed knapsack, slinging his camera case around his neck, and waving goodbye with a grin as he headed toward the immigration counter. "I believe his exact words were, 'I shall take prize-winning photographs as I stroll through charming English villages!' "

"Where do you think he is now?" Michael asked, turning to Kate. He knew she probably had Danny's schedule memorized.

"I think he was planning to be in Scotland today or tomorrow," she answered.The phone rang, and Nonnie hurried inside to answer it. Kate heard her say, "Danny! Where are you calling from?" Kate's heart skipped a beat as she jumped up and hurried into the house.

"It's Danny. He wants to talk to you," Nonnie said, handing her the phone.

"Hi, buddy!" Kate said, a smile wreathing her face. The joy of hearing his voice overshadowed any apprehension about why he might be calling. "How's your trip going?"

"Oh . . . , not too bad." Kate thought she detected a tremor in his voice. Could he be homesick?

"Mom . . . ," Danny paused as if struggling to control his voice, and Kate's heart froze.

"What is it, honey?"

"Something happened, Mom."

"What? What happened? Are you OK?"

"I'm . . . OK. I guess I'm just a little shaken up, that's all."

"What happened, Danny?" Kate asked quietly, trying to be calm.

"Well, yesterday, I took the train to Inverness, but I didn't realize how late it would be when I got here. I asked about a bed-and-breakfast at the station, and the station master called a few, but they were all full. He told me the train stayed in the station all night and I could sleep on it if I wanted to."

Kate murmured her understanding. "So what did you do?"

"Well, a man who had been sitting in the waiting room came over and told me I could stay at his house."

Kate caught her breath. Danny was too innocent and trusting. She realized belatedly that this was the very kind of situation she had unconsciously been worried about.

"And what did you do?" she prodded.

"Well, he seemed like a real nice man, and I thought staying with him would be better than sleeping on the train all night. But, Mom . . . ," Danny's voice dropped almost to a whisper. "Mom, when we got to his house, I found out there was only one bed and we'd have to sleep in it together."

Kate swallowed her rising panic, not wanting to hear the rest of Danny's story. But he went on.

"Mom . . . , he was a homosexual . . ."

Kate realized Danny was crying. The hair stood up on the back of her neck as she fought the urge to claw that man's eyes out, to tear him limb from limb! She raged inwardly at her helplessness to save her child from the world's evil!

"Oh, buddy," she murmured brokenly. "What happened?"

"He didn't do anything to me, Mom," Danny answered quickly. "He wanted to, but I got up and slept in a chair and left real early this morning."

"Danny, why don't you see if you can change your ticket and come home today," Kate urged, longing to see him.

"I'll be OK, Mom. I'm going back to England now. I don't want to stay in Scotland. It's only two more days till I come home. I just needed to hear your voice. Don't you worry, OK?"

"OK," Kate said shakily. "But do be careful!"

"I will," Danny assured her.

"And don't lose your plane ticket!" she added desperately. They had both laughed.

Staring with unseeing eyes at the magazine on her lap, Kate realized that shock had blanked that moment from her mind until now. When they had met Danny at the airport, she remembered looking at him searchingly to see if he had changed, but they had never spoken of it again.

Could that experience have affected Danny? she wondered. Laying the magazine on the lamp table, Kate stood up and headed for the stairs. On impulse, she paused as she passed the desk, opened the top drawer, and pulled out a packet of envelopes. Her mother had saved all the letters she had written from Singapore. Thoughtfully, Kate slipped off the rubber band and opened an envelope. There was something she remembered . . .

Yes, this was the one. "Danny and Julie are inseparable," she had written, "but they do have their problems. Julie always wants to play house, but they both want to be the mommy. Her mother told me the other day that Julie finally let Danny be the mommy, and he was so happy!"

Slowly, Kate folded the letter and slid it back into the envelope. Somewhere, down below the surface of her mind, a frightening suspicion was beginning to grow.

That night, as she tossed and turned, trying to get to sleep, another long-buried memory surfaced. She had been the PTA leader the year Danny was in sixth grade. One day Mr. Gibson, teacher of the upper-grade room, had called to schedule a special PTA meeting. "This will be for the parents only," he stressed. "See if you can get someone to supervise games on the court for the children."

The guest speaker had talked about the growing numbers of openly homosexual men in the States. There was a real danger, he warned, that fathers who traveled extensively and were away from home for long periods of time were setting up their sons for the possibility of becoming homosexuals.

For the most part, Kate remembered, his talk had either been received with indignation or had been laughed off by the fathers present. Some of the mothers had been concerned, but eventually their fears subsided. *Their* boys couldn't have *that* kind of a problem. Now she wondered if she should have taken the warning more seriously. Would God allow such an awful thing to happen as a result of fathers traveling in His work? There seemed to be no answers, only more and more questions.

The next day, Kate stopped at the supermarket to buy salad things on the way home from the office. That evening, as she tore spinach leaves, chopped purple cabbage, and sliced a yellow squash, she felt almost paralyzed by a nameless fear. She couldn't bring herself to articulate it, but down in the murky depths of her subconscious floated a dreaded word.

Kate choked down a few bites of salad, then got up and wandered aimlessly through the house. In the bedroom, she paused. Sitting down on the edge of the bed, she stared at the telephone. Slowly, the conviction grew that she would find the answer in that telephone. At last, with great difficulty, she forced herself to face the terrible question.

Is it possible that Danny could be a homosexual? The question, with all its implications, reverberated in her mind.

She *had* to know about Danny, but she didn't dare ask him outright. What if she were wrong? But how could she find out? Then she thought of the pastor at the college church. Danny and Angela had gone to him for premarital counseling. Clinging to the hope that her suspicions were unfounded, she decided to call and ask him.

Still she hesitated, dreading what she might learn, but at last, she reached out and picked up the receiver. Her hand shook as she dialed the number and listened to it ring. Her heart began to race as she heard a click at the other end of the line.

"College Church, Bob Wright speaking," said a business-like voice.

"Pastor Wright, this is Kate McLaughlin, Danny's mother." Kate paused. Her throat felt so tight she could hardly breathe.

"Uh, Pastor Wright, I know Danny and Angela came to you for premarital counseling. I, uh . . . ," Kate's voice was trembling uncontrollably, and she drew a deep breath, then plunged on.

"I guess you know they've broken their engagement, and lately I have been wondering about Danny. I know you can't tell me anything he told you in confidence, but . . ."

Again, Kate struggled to control her voice. "I have been wondering if Danny could be homosexual. Could you at least tell me if I should talk to him about it?"

There was a long moment of uncomfortable silence while Kate felt sick with dread. Then the pastor answered, rather stiffly, "Yes, you should talk to him. But be very careful not to say anything that might drive him into a lifestyle neither of us would want."

The moment Kate heard his "yes," she clamped her hand over the mouthpiece and began rocking back and forth, moaning softly. When he finished speaking, she hung up without saying goodbye, and a wild cry of grief tore from her throat.

"God! What can I do?" she cried frantically. In a state of shock, she jumped from the bed and began walking blindly through the house, screaming in short, gasping breaths—screams of rage, pain, and disbelief—and pounding her fist against the wall so hard that her arm ached for days afterward.

Back in the bedroom, Kate threw herself on the bed. She felt as if she were sinking into a deep black hole of despair. Sobs shook her body as she cried until there were no more tears left. Dark, torturing questions circled endlessly through her mind, like a whirlpool sucking her deeper and deeper.

Is Danny eternally lost?

Will he die of AIDS?

Is this the end of all our hopes and dreams for him?

Will he never have a wife or children?

Why? Why? WHY?

Is it our fault?

What did we do wrong?

Could we have done something to prevent it?

An hour passed before Kate rolled over and stared blankly at the ceiling, an occasional shuddering breath all that remained of her tears. One last question filled her mind.

What has this been like for Danny?

Chapter 3

What Is a Homosexual?

The room was dark when at last Kate became aware of her surroundings. Slowly, she heaved herself to a sitting position. Everything seemed so unreal. She sat there lethargically, wondering if she would ever have the energy to get up. After several long moments, she dragged herself over to her computer and turned it on.

I have to write to Danny, she thought. *He needs to know that we still love him anyway.*

How could this terrible thing have happened? Danny, a homosexual? But that can't be! Danny's not like that. What is a homosexual, anyway?

What do I really know about homosexuals? Kate wondered. She remembered reading about gay bathhouses in *Newsweek* and seeing men walking arm in arm in a gay-pride march on television. She remembered driving through an area of San Francisco where men walked the streets dressed like women. But she couldn't reconcile these pictures with the gentle, sensitive boy she knew Danny was, in spite of his childhood love for dressing up. Scenes flashed through her mind.

She pictured Danny's bright, eager face on the front row of the children's class at church through all her years of being a leader. He had always been her most enthusiastic participant, the first to respond when she asked for volunteers, a willing pupil when her teachers practiced telling the Bible story.

She remembered how five-year-old Danny had started a Bible Story hour of his own for some of the Chinese children in the neighboring kampong, or village. He and Julie, the little girl next door, had gone down to the kampong to give the children their old church papers. Then Danny began inviting them home so he could teach them songs and tell them Bible stories, using Kate's flannel board. Sometimes he took them for a nature walk, learnedly discoursing on birds, butterflies, and trees. He kept it up for several months, until two of the little girls began attending church with him.

She thought of Danny, at nine, faithfully attending every meeting of a revival series held by a well-known evangelist from the States. When a call was made for those who wanted to give their hearts to God, Danny was one of the first to respond, walking alone to the front of the church. Kate remembered her tears of joy as Michael and Danny stood in the baptistry a year later. Baptizing his three sons had been among the highlights of Michael's life.

Even in high school, Danny had reached out enthusiastically to others, organizing singing groups for the hospital patients, giving out religious literature in the neighboring high-rises, or being involved in other witnessing activities.

How is it possible that Danny could be so sensitive to spiritual things and also be a homosexual? Kate wondered. She realized that she had always thought of homosexuals as being perverted, obsessed with sex, but that picture couldn't be completely accurate if Danny was a homosexual.

Kate had always felt especially close to Danny because of the love they shared for music, writing, art, and poetry. How could she *not* have known? What signs had there been that she had missed? Had he been attracted to boys before?

Kate's forehead wrinkled in concentration as she tried to remember. Danny had dated in high school. With a smile, she recalled the Boys' Club banquet during his freshman year at the small boarding school for missionaries' children in Singapore. There had been more girls than boys, and Danny, waiting until all the other boys had dates, had asked the nine girls who were left if he could escort them. He had given each of them a long-stemmed red rose, and Danny and his dates had been seated at a table in the center of the room.

Danny had always had lots of good friends who were girls, but, Kate now realized, they had been more like sisters than romantic interests. Except for Angela. Surely she had seen tenderness and love between Danny and Angela.

But there *had* been boys. . . . When Alex graduated from academy and returned to the States for college, they had all missed him, but it had been especially hard on Danny. And then, two years later, Brenden had left for college too, and Danny had really been lonesome with both his brothers gone.

Even though he was only twelve at the time, he began hanging around the older high-school students. And soon Kate began to hear a lot about Melvin, a high-school junior, one of the spiritual leaders in the school, a nice boy in every way. He took Danny under his wing. Kate was glad Danny had found someone to take the place of his brothers.

Two years later, when Danny started high school, he became especially attached to Kevin, a senior who was a solid Christian, a good student, and one of the school leaders. Kate remembered that she had been happy Danny chose such good friends. After Kevin graduated, Danny's best friend had been Mitch. And then, in his senior year, there had been Max. At the time, Kate had thought they were just special friends, but now she wondered. Had there been something more in Danny's feelings for these boys?

With an effort, Kate brought her thoughts back to the present. She stared at her blank computer screen. What could she say to Danny? Had he been struggling with unacceptable feelings for years without her being aware of it? How did he feel now? What had Pastor Wright meant about not pushing him into a lifestyle neither of them would want? What *was* a homosexual, anyway? Clearly, she needed to learn more about homosexuality, because her preconceived ideas did not seem to fit the picture.

For now, she forced herself to concentrate on the task at hand. "Dear Danny," she finally typed. "For several days a question has been heavy on my heart, but I could not find the courage to ask you. This afternoon I finally decided to call Pastor Wright. I told him what I suspected and asked him if

I should talk to you about it. Before I say anymore, I want to tell you that I love you with all my heart, and nothing can ever change that.

"Oh, Danny, my heart aches so for you. I know that you must have struggled and agonized over this for a long time. I wish it hadn't taken me so long to see it, but maybe you can understand that my natural inclination was to deny the hints as long as possible. If only I had recognized it sooner, maybe we could have worked it through before it became so big.

"Danny, you don't have to face this alone. If you are willing, I think it would be good for us to talk this over openly and honestly. Maybe it would help both of us to understand why and how this has happened. I guess some people think this is something that can't be changed, but others believe it can be if you are willing to let God help.

"Danny, whatever happens, I hope you won't come to the place where you give up and decide to change to another lifestyle. God CAN save us from any sin that enslaves us if we let Him. And as much as Daddy and I love you, God loves you so much more."

Tears were streaming down Kate's face as she printed the letter and put it in an envelope. She longed to see Danny right now, to find out what he was thinking and feeling, but she would have to wait.

The next day, Kate had difficulty concentrating on her work. She felt numb, but at the same time, she felt an urgent need to learn more about homosexuality. She had no idea how to go about it. She certainly couldn't talk to anyone. Homosexuality was simply not a subject that was discussed by her circle of friends.

She didn't even know where to look for a book about it, and if she found one, she didn't think she would have the nerve to buy it or check it out of a library.

After lunch she had to deliver a report to someone upstairs. Suddenly, she had an idea.

Trying to appear more casual than she felt, Kate poked her head in the door of the Family Life office. Jennie, the director's secretary, was standing at the file cabinet.

"Hi, Jennie," Kate greeted her. "I have a problem. Maybe you can help me. I have a friend who just found out her son is gay. She's terribly upset, and I thought maybe I could find something for her to read that would help. Can you give me any suggestions?" Kate was amazed at the ease with which her request slipped out.

"Sure, Kate," Jennie answered sympathetically, straightening up and going over to a tall cupboard at one end of the office. "We have some material here in the department." She took out a small booklet and some mimeographed pages and handed them to Kate.

"There's a bibliography at the end of this, if she would like to get some more information. And tell your friend she's not alone. A lot of parents in our church have gone through the same thing. She's lucky she has you to talk to. Most people feel like there's nobody they can talk to."

"Thanks. I'll tell her," replied Kate, feeling a twinge of conscience at her misrepresentation. Suddenly self-conscious, she quickly said goodbye and slipped away. She could hardly wait till time to go home so she could read the material Jennie had given her.

When she left the office that afternoon, Kate scarcely noticed the thick gray clouds overhead or the damp spring breeze that whipped at her jacket as she hurried to the car. Driving home, she thought about Jennie's remark, "A lot of parents in our church have gone through the same thing." Somehow, there was comfort in knowing she was not the only one facing this heartache. But how would she ever be able to find anyone who shared her sorrow? She couldn't imagine ever having the courage to talk openly about it. And if there were others, they must feel the same way.

When she got home, Kate hurried into the house. Quickly she changed into her comfortable robe and slippers, poured a glass of milk, and dropped into Michael's favorite chair expectantly. At last she could begin to understand what had happened to Danny.

As rain beat furiously at the window, she turned on the

lamp against the sudden gloom. She picked up the little green booklet. The title, in yellow letters, read *Freedom From Homosexuality*. She turned to the first page.

"This book is for the person who wants to be released from the prison of homosexuality. I have experienced this freedom myself for the past eight years," Kate read. That certainly sounded hopeful!

She read on as she sipped at her milk. "You can change your feelings and behavior by changing your way of thinking." Kate frowned. Surely Danny's problem wasn't caused by wrong thinking, was it?

Homosexuality, the author declared, was really an unconscious effort to find the affection and closeness that a person had not experienced with his father as a child. In addition, he continued, the hurt from not getting the love he needed caused a person to feel unworthy of love and to block any further possibility of receiving love, for fear of being hurt again. As a result, he never found his identity as a man. And not only did he block out human love, but God's love as well, distorting his spiritual, as well as emotional, thinking.

Kate drew a deep breath. It sounded logical, but did it fit Danny's situation? While she couldn't deny that Michael had been gone a lot during Danny's childhood, it was difficult to believe that Danny had felt unloved by him.

Reading further, Kate grew more comfortable as the author placed homosexuality squarely within the conflict between the powers of good and evil, presenting God's grace as the power that could overthrow Satan's forces, which caused homosexuality. The homosexual, he said, must exercise faith and believe that God had created him as a heterosexual, even though he did not feel like one. "Celebrate your sexuality!" he urged. "It is not your sexuality that is sin, but your misuse of it."

When she had finished reading the booklet, Kate forgot her earlier misgivings. She would have to show it to Danny. Surely he would be happy to realize that there was a way out.

As Kate took her glass to the kitchen, she passed Danny and Angela's quilt, still on its frame in front of the window, where it had been sitting untouched since the day Danny had called to announce his broken engagement.

Putting her glass in the sink, Kate slowly retraced her steps until she stood looking down at the quilt. She reached out to touch it, and sudden tears rained down as a storm of weeping shook her. She dropped into the rocking chair beside the quilt until her tears subsided.

She began to rock as she gazed at the symbol of her broken dreams. At last, with a sigh, she loosened the quilt from its frame, shook it out, and gently folded it. Climbing the stairs, she laid it carefully in the bottom of her carved teak blanket chest. A bleak feeling of desolation swept her, as if she had buried a dream.

Sunday was family phone day. Kate wondered if Danny had gotten her letter. Would he call, or should she call him? After lunch she decided she couldn't wait any longer and dialed Danny's dorm room.

"Hi, Danny. How are you?" Kate hoped her voice sounded normal.

"Hi, Mom. I'm fine."

Hesitantly, she asked, "Did you get my letter?"

"Yeah."

After Danny's noncommittal response, Kate paused. "Danny, how did it make you feel?"

Danny was silent for a long moment. "Well, I was pretty shaken up at first, but now I guess I'm glad you found out without my having to tell you. Actually, I've been trying to get up my nerve to tell you for quite a while, but I kept putting it off. I . . ." Danny hesitated. "Are you going to tell Dad?"

"Do you want me to? Or would you rather tell him?"

"I'm not sure I'm ready yet. But if you think he needs to know, I guess it's OK with me if you want to tell him."

"Well, maybe we'll play it by ear," Kate said uneasily. "Danny, I've been wondering . . . , have you talked to a pastor or anybody about this?"

"Mom, I know you're just finding out about it, but I've known I was different ever since I was a little boy," Danny answered with a hint of impatience in his voice. "Yes, I spent many hours discussing it with Pastor Carson in high school, and I have talked to one of the Bible teachers here at college quite a bit.

"Mom, ever since I was in seventh grade and found out the name for what was different about me, I have prayed and prayed that God would change me, but He hasn't, so I have finally had to accept myself for what I am so I can get on with the business of living."

Tears filled Kate's eyes at the pain and hurt Danny expressed. "Oh, Danny, I don't know very much about this, but I believe with all my heart that God loves you and wants to help you. Please don't give up on God."

"Well, I don't think I have given up on God, but I have to believe that since He didn't change me, He understands that I'm the way I am. I didn't ask to be this way, and I sure spent a lot of years of my life trying to change, but I can't waste the rest of my life that way. I've got to be who I am." Kate was startled by the ragged edge of anger in Danny's voice.

After a pause, he continued, "But, Mom, I want you to know how glad I am to know you still love me." His voice faltered. "I was sure you would, but I was afraid to test it."

"Oh, Danny," Kate said with a sob, "of course I still love you. This doesn't change anything. You're still my dear son, and I'm praying for you every minute." Kate blew her nose. "Have you gotten your plane ticket for next week?"

"Yeah," Danny answered. "I'm supposed to get in at Dulles about 8:30. The flight to BWI was full. . . . Will Dad be home?"

"No, he's still in South America and won't get back for two weeks yet. Danny, maybe we can talk some more while you're home."

"OK. 'Bye, Mom. It'll be good to see you."

" 'Bye, Danny," Kate said. Then, with a desperate attempt to bring everything back to normal, she added, "And don't lose your plane ticket!"

Danny's welcome laughter rang in Kate's ears as she hung up.

Chapter 4

Spring Break

Kate maneuvered her white Honda somewhat distractedly through the evening traffic on Route 66 as she watched for the airport exit. Mingled anticipation and apprehension made her stomach jumpy.

She glanced at her watch as the soaring roofline of Dulles International Airport came into view. She still had ten minutes before Danny's flight was scheduled to arrive. Nosing her car into the first parking space she could find, she grabbed her purse, jumped out, locked the door, and walked quickly toward the terminal.

Stopping to check the monitor near the door, she hurried on to Gate 11 and positioned herself where she could see down the jetway. She nibbled at her thumbnail anxiously.

At some subconscious level, Kate felt as if she were meeting a stranger. It was a shock to realize that this son, whom she thought she had known like her own heartbeat, had for years hidden a whole dimension of himself from her.

Soon, the first passengers began striding up the ramp. Kate drew a deep breath and strained to see a familiar face. And then, there he was, in his gray slacks, white shirt, and sleeveless burgundy sweater. Kate's heart suddenly lifted like a helium-filled balloon as she realized that he was still the same beloved son she had always known.

"Mom!" Danny called with a wide grin. He dashed past the other passengers and grabbed her in a warm bearhug.

"How was your trip?" Kate asked eagerly, as relief that he

hadn't changed coursed through her.

"Great! I finished reading *Perelandra.*"

"Good. Maybe I can read it again while you're home." Kate smiled, remembering how Danny had introduced her to the C. S. Lewis Space Trilogy. "Did you have a good meal?"

"Hey, I ordered a fruit plate! I'll never go vegetarian again! No more overcooked asparagus or soggy potatoes for me. It was delicious. Strawberries, orange slices, and grapes. With bread, crackers, and cheese. You ought to try it sometime."

"I will," laughed Kate. "Now let's go get your stuff."

They chattered nonstop all the way home.

As they turned into the driveway, Danny looked at the gray house flanked by evergreens—the home he had not been sure would welcome him with his new identity. "It's *good* to be home," he exclaimed fervently, adding softly, "I'm glad I have a home to come to." Kate's throat tightened.

"Do you want anything to eat?" she asked as she unlocked the door, covering her emotion with the mundane question.

"How about some popcorn? I don't think I've had any since I was home last summer."

"OK," she said, heading for the kitchen to get out the popper.

Danny dropped his suitcase by the door. "Have you missed me, piano?" he asked, sliding onto the piano bench.

"I've tried to keep it from getting too lonesome," Kate called from the kitchen.

Danny's fingers coaxed a Brahm's *Intermezzo* from the keys as Kate smiled contentedly. For a while, she could almost imagine that the last two weeks had just been a nightmare.

A few minutes later, a delicious aroma filled the air as Kate came into the living room carrying two bowls of fluffy white popcorn. Setting one on the piano for Danny, she curled up in a corner of the couch with the other.

"Tell me about the passion play," she urged.

Danny stopped playing and swung around on the bench to face her. "It was the best one we've ever put on," he said enthusiastically. "Over a thousand people came to see it. The crucifixion scene was especially good. Angie directed it."

A strangeness settled over Kate at the mention of Angela's name. "What does Angela think about . . . *this*?" she asked slowly.

"You mean about me being gay? She's known about it ever since we met at camp," Danny said, somewhat impatiently.

"But . . . I don't understand . . ." Kate groped her way carefully. "If Angela knew, why . . . ?"

"We went to town together on our first day off," Danny remembered, giving a short laugh. "Of all things, we ended up in a stationery store looking at wedding invitations. I told her I thought I was gay, and she told me she thought I probably just hadn't met the right girl yet.

"By the end of the summer, I was beginning to wonder if maybe she was the right girl. It was such a relief! It seemed like the answer to all my problems. I could make everybody happy."

"Then, why . . . ?"

"Mom, I finally had to admit that it just wasn't enough. I needed something . . . *more*, something *different*. Something Angie couldn't give me."

"Oh, Danny," Kate said eagerly, "I think there's hope. I've just read the most wonderful booklet. It's by a Christian who used to be gay. God has healed him, and now he has a ministry to help other homosexuals. His name is Chuck Carlson, and . . ."

"Forget it, Mom!" Danny interrupted with a bitter vehemence that startled Kate. "Haven't you heard about him? All the time he was supposed to be helping gays become straight, he was actually seducing them!"

Kate's mouth dropped open. "Oh no, Danny, surely not!" she said in dismay. "Why would the Family Life office be using his book if that were true? Where did you hear that?"

"It's true, Mom. Some of the guys who went through his program have just recently accused him of this, so maybe not everybody in the church has heard about it yet, but he doesn't deny that they are telling the truth."

Disappointment flooded over Kate like the shock of a cold

shower as she realized how much she had pinned her hopes on this being the answer—the solution that would make everything right again. Tears stung her eyes as she tried to find something to say. At last, she said slowly, "Well, Danny, I'm sorry that he betrayed the trust of those who came to him for help, but human beings have failures; that's why we need a Saviour. I still believe that he had the right idea."

"No, Mom, he was wrong!" Danny exclaimed in disgust. "It's just plain cruel to hold out the hope that you can change and become heterosexual! If God was going to change anybody, He should have changed me, because I prayed for years that He would."

Tears spilled down Kate's cheeks. "Oh, Danny, I don't know what to say, but there must be an answer. Let's keep praying about it."

Danny shook the unpopped kernels in his bowl but didn't answer. Kate brushed the tears away with the back of her hand. At last, with a deep sigh, she said, "Well, buddy, I expect you're tired. Let's go to bed, and maybe things will look brighter in the morning."

Getting up from the couch, Kate walked over to Danny and put her arm around his shoulders. Danny looked up at her with a sad little smile. "I love you, Mom," he said soberly.

Danny was still sleeping the next morning when Kate looked in on him before leaving. She paused in the doorway and studied her son's face. Yes, he still looked the same: glossy, dark brown hair; trim little mustache; long lashes against the smooth curve of cheek; and his pride and joy, a carefully cropped beard. How dear he was! And yet, she now realized, under the surface of his warm, witty, affectionate personality, he bore the scars of a long and painful struggle.

Kate had a busy morning at work, with no time to think about anything else. She had just gotten back to her office after giving a staff education presentation when the phone rang.

"Hi, Mom. Where do you keep the yeast? I'm going to bake some bread."

"Yummy! Why don't you make some of your special

raisin-walnut bread," Kate said. "The yeast should be on the bottom shelf of the refrigerator door. By the way, I left some split pea soup in the fridge for your lunch, and there are some muffins in the bread drawer."

The year Danny was in fifth grade, Kate remembered, his teacher had decided that the boys and girls would switch their regular practical-arts classes. The girls took woodworking and the boys, cooking. Danny had thoroughly enjoyed it, bringing home some new delicacy every week. He developed into such a good bread maker that he later got a job baking bread for the high-school cafeteria.

When Kate got home that evening, she sniffed appreciatively as she opened the door. "I might have known you'd make chocolate-chip cookies too," she chuckled.

"And . . . I made spaghetti and a big tossed salad for dinner!" Danny said with a flourish. "Whew! I'm tired! I've been cooking all day."

Kate raised an eyebrow as she glanced around the kitchen. "I can believe it! Well, the maid's here now to clean up the mess, so go sit down and rest!" She punched his shoulder playfully.

Danny left the room but soon came back and perched on a stool as Kate set about restoring the kitchen to order. Stacking dishes in the sink, she wondered how to bring up the subject that stood like a wall between them.

"Does Angela's mother know why you broke up?" she asked after a bit, polishing the stove vigorously.

Danny shifted on his stool. "No, Angie doesn't want her to know," he said at last. "She's terribly prejudiced against homosexuals, and Angie is afraid she would try to cause trouble for me."

"But she really loves you," protested Kate.

"She wouldn't if she knew I was gay," insisted Danny. "I've heard her say some terrible things about gays. It would probably make her furious if she thought I had deceived her."

Thoughtfully, Kate put the flour, sugar, and cinnamon back in the cupboard. "I don't know, Danny. I think maybe you're misjudging her."

"Well, I don't think I want to find out. And Angie would be upset if you told her," he warned.

"Oh, I won't tell her," promised Kate. "But she's called us a couple of times, you know, and she feels so bad about it. She keeps hoping you'll get back together."

Danny heaved a big sigh. "Angie will just have to handle her," he said, reaching into the cookie jar.

"Hey, stay out of those till after we eat!" exclaimed Kate, laughing.

Dinner over, Danny pushed his chair back and stood up. "Could I borrow the car this evening?" he asked casually. "I called Jim this afternoon, and he wants me to come over."

"Sure," Kate answered automatically. "The keys are in my purse. I'll get them for you." But as she walked down the hall to her bedroom, doubt suddenly seized her. *Why is Danny going to see Jim?*

Jim was the assistant manager of the college radio station, where Danny had worked the year he had stayed home and attended a nearby college. *Could he and Danny . . . ? What should I do? Is there really any reason for my suspicions? I don't want to accuse Danny of something, when maybe there's nothing. I have to trust him, don't I? I can't just say, "No, you can't see Jim." Anyway, Jim has a car, and if he and Danny want to get together, they'll do it, whether I forbid it or not.*

Kate got the keys out of her purse and went back to the kitchen. "Just don't stay out too late," she said, handing them to Danny. "You know I can't sleep till you get home."

"Aw, Mom! I'm not a baby anymore," exclaimed Danny. "Thanks for the car. I'll try to get home early."

As Kate stood by the window and watched the red taillights disappear down the street, she tried to ignore the doubts that assailed her. At last, she turned away and walked back to the kitchen, making an effort to put all questions out of her mind.

The clock on her night stand said 11:32 when Kate heard Danny turn the key in the front door. Now she could relax. But sleep still eluded her, as thoughts she didn't dare listen to buzzed around in her head. Finally, she got out of bed and slipped to her knees.

"Father, You know how worried I am about Danny. I don't understand all of this. I don't know what to do. But you know how to help him. And I know You love him too, even more than I do. Please take care of him. Oh, Father, I love him so!"

Tears wet her pillow, but Kate quickly fell asleep.

The following Sunday, Kate woke up to a resplendent spring morning. It was impossible to feel sad or depressed on such a day. The sky was a brilliant azure blue, and the blossoming pear trees that bordered the street looked like billowing white clouds as they tossed in the breeze. A double row of yellow tulips edged the drive.

Kate pulled on a pair of jeans and a sweat shirt and tied her sneakers. "Wake up, you sleepyhead! Get up! Get out of bed!" she sang, poking her head in Danny's door. "It's too beautiful a morning to waste in bed. Come take a walk with me."

"Aw, Mom," grumbled Danny sleepily. Kate came in and pulled the blanket back.

"OK! OK!" Danny said reluctantly, sitting up and throwing his pillow at her.

"Come on," urged Kate. "I'll pour you a glass of orange juice."

Ten minutes later, they crossed the street and walked briskly around the park. "There's a robin!" exclaimed Kate. "Spring is really here."

When they got back home, Kate fixed Danny's favorite breakfast—slices of toast, thickly spread with peanut butter and topped with warm applesauce. As she looked at him sitting across from her, joking and laughing, everything seemed so normal, so good. Yet a strange feeling of unreality cast a shadow over her spirit.

"Danny," she said, as he forked a bite into his mouth, "remember that time when you called us from Scotland? Did . . . Do you think . . ." She tried again. "Well, could that experience have had any influence on you?"

Danny gazed out the window as he chewed. He swallowed and turned back to Kate. "Mom, I told you before, this is something I've known about myself for a long time. I can't remember a time when I didn't realize I was different.

"That time in Scotland, . . . it was something I wanted to happen, in a way, . . . but when it did, I was scared. I wanted to find out if I really . . ." He took a deep breath and released it. "It was such an overpowering feeling. It was an unmistakable confirmation of what I am.

"You know, when I worked at that publishing company after camp was over, the summer before my freshman year— my boss there was gay. I knew about it, but I never told him about myself. But when I went back there and worked during spring break, I decided to tell him. I'm not sure why. I didn't want to get involved with him or anything, but there was something exciting about being able to talk about it with somebody who could understand me.

"I don't know exactly how to describe it . . ." Danny paused, searching for words. "I guess I always felt kind of like a black man living in a white community. I always felt cut off, alienated, from everybody around me. So, when I found somebody whom I could identify with, who really knew how I felt at the core of my being, it was an incredibly liberating experience."

Kate could hardly swallow past the lump in her throat. A feeling of profound sadness for the pain and confusion she had never recognized in Danny's life overwhelmed her. When she could talk, she said softly, "Oh, Danny, I am so sorry. If only I had known what you were going through, maybe I could have done something to help."

"Don't feel bad, Mom," Danny said with a gentle smile. "You did a great job of raising me, and I have lots of wonderful memories. I wouldn't have wanted you to know. It was something I could never have talked to you about."

On the way to the airport that afternoon, Kate felt as if she were trying to balance on a tightrope—wanting to show Danny that her love for him was as strong as ever, yet not wanting him to think she could possibly condone what she felt was a sinful lifestyle. As she waved goodbye, Kate wondered if she could have believed, years ago, that being a parent could bring this much pain.

Chapter 5

How Will I Tell Michael?

Sitting in her office, Kate suddenly realized that she had been staring at her computer screen for an unknown length of time while confused, troubled thoughts whirled through her mind. Tears filled her eyes as a feeling of unbearable sadness rolled over her.

"Here's your morning mail, my dear." Kate jumped as she heard Sally's voice behind her, and she reached quickly for a tissue.

"What's the matter, honey?" Sally exclaimed in a concerned voice. "Allergies?"

"Could be," Kate hedged, trying to smile as she wiped her eyes and blew her nose.

"Mine have been bad this year too," Sally sympathized. "I have to run. I'm in the middle of a big project." She patted Kate on the shoulder as she turned to go. "Take care of yourself, dear. I hope you feel better tomorrow."

"Thanks," Kate said weakly.

Since Danny had left, the numbness that followed the first shock of finding out about his homosexuality had begun to wear off. As the sharp pain of reality overwhelmed Kate, she gradually sank into a deep depression. At home she found herself pacing restlessly around the house or rummaging through the cupboards looking for something to eat, instead of busily filling every minute with quilting, reading, playing the piano, or walking, as she had done before—a lifetime ago. Kate had never been one to cry easily, but now tears came unbidden at the slightest provocation.

Worst of all were the nights, when her courage was at its lowest ebb. Then the demons of guilt and despair stalked her thoughts, and sleep evaded her.

Is it my fault Danny's a homosexual? she wondered. Somewhere she had heard that it was caused by possessive, domineering mothers. But the book by Chuck Carlson seemed to indicate that a problem in the relationship with the father was the cause.

Yes, Michael was away on many long trips while Danny was growing up, Kate thought, as her subconscious mind desperately tried to place the blame on someone else. Four-to six-week itineraries were the norm for church administrators. *He missed so many of the boys' birthdays. It seems as though he was always traveling when they had a special school program.* Of course, it was what the church expected of its leaders.

But if Michael's absences made Danny homosexual, then why aren't Alex and Brenden homosexual too? argued another part of her mind. *For that matter, the other fathers on the mission compound were away just as often as Michael, and their boys didn't turn out to be gay.*

Kate remembered something else. Michael had always found it difficult to understand Danny's disinterest in sports. He couldn't fathom a boy who would prefer reading Shakespeare or writing poems to playing baseball. Could this incompatibility have made Danny homosexual? Or was his lack of interest in typical masculine pursuits simply a sign of his orientation?

Maybe it was my fault, after all. Was I domineering? Kate tried to be objective. *I have to admit I did my share of nagging about homework and chores. But was it more than normal? I really don't think so. And Michael and I never tried to tell any of our boys what career to choose.*

Was I possessive? Again, Kate struggled to be honest. *Overprotective, maybe.* She was a worrier, she knew. When Michael or the boys were late getting home, her overactive imagination began picturing the worst. She had often reminded them to call her if they were going to be late. She tried to keep her fears to herself, but she knew she hadn't been very successful. *Still, that's different from being possessive*, she decided. *I always tried to let my boys make their own decisions, and I don't think I got overinvolved in their lives.*

On the other hand, she realized, there *had* been a special bond between Danny and her because of their shared interests. In some ways, Danny had taken the place of the daughter she had never had. He enjoyed working in the kitchen with her and liked to set the table beautifully with her good china when they had company.

And more than either of his brothers, Danny had shared her love for classical music, her fascination with words, and her passion for poetry. Kate had known very few who seemed to care about the artistic side of life as much as she did. Had her delight in Danny's compatibility been abnormal or wrong?

At this point in Kate's tortured thoughts, guilt always overwhelmed her. Could their relationship, which had seemed so good, so fulfilling, have brought about such heartache? Kate's burden of guilt grew heavier each day.

Compounding it was another question. For many years, Kate had struggled with a food-dependency problem. She had developed the habit of turning to food for comfort when she was lonely, discouraged, depressed, or bored. Eating had become a way of coping with just about any negative emotion. She had tried countless times to overcome this habit, which, she was well aware, was self-destructive and sinful, but she had failed again and again. Could this weakness, this character defect, have anything to do with causing Danny's problem?

The day Michael was to arrive home, Kate arose exhausted from another restless night. *How will I tell Michael about Danny?* she wondered with a heavy heart. A thread of worry and uncertainty wove itself uneasily through her thoughts all day.

It seemed as if the day would never end, and yet, as she headed home from the office that evening, Michael's arrival seemed to be rushing toward her. She busied herself with straightening up the house, then lay down on the bed, trying to concentrate on the new quilting magazine that had just come in the mail.

When car headlights shone through her bedroom window that evening, Kate hurried to the door in a flood of mingled dread and relief.

"Oh, honey, it seems like you've been gone forever!" she exclaimed, throwing her arms around Michael's neck.

Michael dropped his bags and planted a hungry kiss on her lips. "It was a good trip, but am I ever glad to be home!" he said fervently. He turned and glanced around the yard. "Looks like spring came while I was gone."

"Yes, you may even have to mow the lawn pretty soon," laughed Kate, pushing aside the thoughts that had been tormenting her.

As usual when he returned from a trip, Michael was eager to tell her about all his exciting experiences as they unpacked his bags. It was late when they got to bed. In the quiet after Michael fell asleep, Kate realized that there had been no convenient opportunity to talk with him about Danny.

Her eyes were closed, but she was not asleep as she lay perfectly still on the bed beside Michael. She heard the ticking of the grandfather clock in the living room, the faraway barking of a dog, a car passing on the street outside. It seemed as if she had been lying in the same position for hours. She suddenly realized that her hands were clenched, every muscle was rigid and taut, and she was holding her breath. With a deep sigh, she rolled over on her side and tried to relax.

But sleep would not come. Every time she started to relax, the terrible, unbelievable truth would jolt her into frozen wakefulness again.

She looked over at Michael, sleeping peacefully beside her. *He has so many heavy responsibilities; it wouldn't be fair to add this tragedy to his load, would it? How will he be able to handle it?*

And it wasn't just Michael's feelings she had to worry about. *How will he react to Danny? Will he try to understand, or will he be so angry he'll reject Danny? Will his hurt be so great he'll say something that could destroy their relationship?*

Maybe he'll blame me, say it's my fault, that I've been an overprotective mother. Can I take that on top of this constant sorrow? Kate ached with the desperate need to tell Michael, to have someone to talk to about it, but she was so afraid he wouldn't understand.

When the pearly light of approaching day began to brighten the window, Kate climbed wearily out of bed. Picking up her Bible from the bedside table, she slowly dragged herself into the living room and curled up in the corner of the couch.

Through eyes that felt a hundred years old, she looked at the azaleas exploding in bursts of crimson, cerise, and magenta under the dogwood trees. Spring could no longer awaken her excitement; her soul felt numb and dead.

She turned the pages of her Bible and looked at some of the verses she had highlighted in the past few weeks.

> I am worn out from groaning; all night long I flood my bed with weeping and drench my couch with tears (Psalm 6:6).
> Be merciful to me, O Lord; for I am in distress; my eyes grow weak with sorrow, my soul and my body with grief (Psalm 31:9).

Yes, Kate thought, *now I can understand David. I know how he was feeling.* She leafed through several more pages and paused at another verse highlighted in yellow.

> Though you have made me see troubles, many and bitter, you will restore my life again (Psalm 71:20).

That's a ray of hope down in this black pit of despair, she sighed. A few pages farther on, she came upon two verses that made her eyes fill with tears.

As a father has compassion on his children, so the Lord has compassion on those who fear him; for he knows how we are formed, he remembers that we are dust (Psalm 103:13,14).

Oh, Father, she wept, *You must know how devastating this is. Not just to me, but to Danny too. You must feel our sorrow and despair. I cannot understand why this has happened, but I have to believe that You have a way to take care of even this situation.*

Two weeks passed, and still Kate had not brought herself to talk to Michael. Every night she lay awake for hours. Fatigue was a constant companion as she struggled through each day. She was having more and more difficulty concentrating, both at work and at home. She had forgotten important appointments, and last week she had run out of gas on the freeway, something that had never happened to her before. She frequently had the sensation of a heavy weight pressing on her chest, making it difficult to breathe. Still, she somehow managed to hide her distress. Michael didn't seem to notice anything amiss. One morning, when she had the panicky feeling that she couldn't keep going any longer, Kate picked up the phone and made an appointment with Dr. Zimmerman for her annual physical, although it wasn't due for another month. Joyce, the nurse, was able to work her in the next afternoon.

"Your blood pressure is elevated," Dr. Zimmerman commented as he removed the cuff after rechecking Joyce's reading. "Joyce tells me you haven't been feeling too well. What seems to be the problem?"

The sympathetic tone of his inquiry undid Kate. She was just too tired to care what anyone thought. Closing her eyes, she simply let the tears come.

"I thought something was the matter when I first saw you," Dr. Zimmerman said gently, handing Kate a tissue. "Can you tell me about it?"

Kate mopped up, blew her nose, and said in a flat monotone, "I found out two months ago that Danny is homosexual."

"That's tough, Kate! I'm sure it's tough. That's enough stress to play all kinds of havoc with your body. Have you talked to anyone about it yet?"

Kate shook her head.

"Does Michael know?"

Again, she shook her head.

"Kate, you cannot keep this inside!" Dr. Zimmerman spoke firmly. "Promise me you will tell Michael right away. You probably think you're protecting him, but you don't think straight in a situation like this. Michael wouldn't want you trying to handle this by yourself. That's what marriage is all about—sharing and supporting each other in the bad times as well as in the good."

Looking searchingly at her, he added, "And I would strongly recommend that you get some counseling to help you through this."

Kate looked up at that. "Michael has a thing about psychiatrists," she said hesitantly. "Maybe I could talk to our pastor."

"I can go along with that," agreed Dr. Zimmerman. "But don't wait any longer. Your body can't take it. Promise?"

With a wobbly smile, Kate nodded.

Dr. Zimmerman lowered himself to the round black stool beside the examining table and rested his hands on his knees.

"Kate," he said earnestly, "I expect you feel very much alone in this, but there are a lot of others who share your heartache. You know, according to some estimates, around 10 percent of the population has a homosexual orientation. And I don't think the percentage is any different in our church. Among my patients, alone, I know of at least a dozen church families who are affected.

"The hardest part, especially for church members, is that we've been conditioned to think homosexuality is a sin, when it's really homosexual behavior that the Bible is talking about. Even though there is still no conclusive evidence about the exact cause of a person's orientation, we know today that the homosexual has no choice or control over it.

"But most church members don't realize this, so homosexuals and their families feel isolated in shame. I wish we could be more open and supportive of our members who have this heartache."

He stood, then, and pushed the stool out of the way with his foot. He sighed heavily. "Well, Kate, I'll be praying for you and Michael and for Danny too."

Dr. Zimmerman patted Kate's shoulder as he left the room, and this touch of human comfort warmed her heart.

As she drove home, Kate thought about her promise to tell Michael. In one way, the decision brought relief, but she also dreaded it. She tried to plan what she would say, but nothing sounded right. All she could decide was that she would do it that evening after supper.

Michael was describing plans for a booklet he wanted to produce as he helped her clear the table. "I don't think you're listening to me," he declared.

With a clatter, Kate dropped a stack of dishes in the sink. "Michael, I have to tell you something. Come in the living room." Taking his hand, she pulled him to a chair and sat down across from him.

"Michael, I know why Danny broke up with Angela."

Michael looked startled. "Why?"

"I found out that Danny is . . ." Kate swallowed hard as Michael waited expectantly.

"Danny is . . . a homosexual." Kate almost ducked, expecting some kind of explosion, but Michael was just looking at her quizzically.

She rushed on, her words tumbling over each other. "He told me he always felt like he was different. He said when he was about twelve he realized how he was different, but he kept trying to be normal. He dated girls, but he didn't feel the way other boys seemed to feel about them. And for years . . ." Kate's voice broke.

"For years, he said, he prayed that God would change him. When he first met Angela, he told her he thought he was gay before their first date. But she kept telling him he just hadn't met the right girl yet. And after a while, he began to think maybe she was the right girl. He said he really loved Angela, and he was so happy, because he thought marrying her would solve all his problems.

"But he continued to have doubts. He said he still felt attracted to men, and even though he loved Angela, something was missing. He said when their wedding plans began to escalate and it was almost time to order the invitations, he knew he couldn't go through with it. He knew it wouldn't be fair to Angela. . . ." Kate's voice trailed off. She had certainly expected some kind of outraged expression from Michael by now.

"How long have you known about this?" he asked in an ordinary voice.

"About two months," she answered hesitantly.

"Kate, why in the world didn't you tell me right away?" At last, a touch of exasperation colored his voice. "What did you think I would do? You didn't need to hide this from me."

Kate felt relief beginning to flood over her, until Michael continued, "I don't really think this is anything to get too excited about. A lot of boys go through a period of mixed-up sexual feelings during their teens. It's just a phase that some young men go through. But Danny is such a sensitive young man that he has probably talked himself into thinking he is homosexual, when he really isn't."

Kate looked at him in surprise. "But, Michael, I talked to Dr. Zimmerman about it when I had my physical today, and he didn't say anything like that."

A look of annoyance crossed Michael's face. "Kate, you don't need to say anything about this to anybody. You're just getting all upset for no reason. Look, I'll try to talk to Danny, and if I can't convince him, maybe we'll even have to send him to a counselor. Just don't worry about it, OK?"

"OK," Kate said doubtfully. At least she didn't have any more secrets from Michael, but it still didn't look as though she would be able to share her fears with him.

Chapter 6

Is Danny Going to Be Lost?

Danny sat at a desk cluttered with stacks of books, papers, pencils, and a box of raisins. His elbows straddled a large textbook, his chin rested on his fists, and his forehead wrinkled as he squinted at the page in front of him, trying to memorize salient points about the Reformation for an upcoming final exam.

Suddenly his concentration was broken by the shrill ring of the telephone on his dresser. Startled, his head jerked up, and he pushed back his chair to answer it.

"Yeah."

"Hello, Danny."

"Dad!" Danny wrapped his arms protectively around his chest and leaned against the dresser.

"Danny, I was wondering how you're doing. Mom talked to me a couple of days ago, and she told me about you," Michael said awkwardly. "I'm so sorry."

An uncomfortable silence hung in the air between them.

"You know, Danny, a lot of young men go through a phase where they might wonder if they are homosexual, but it doesn't mean they really are. I think maybe you have talked yourself into thinking you might be homosexual because of some feelings or experiences you've had." Michael paused. When no response from Danny was forthcoming, he went on.

"You really should consider very carefully the results of any decisions you might make," he warned. "Your career, for instance. If anybody heard you were a homosexual, you'd never be able to get a job teaching. And you would be asking for all kinds of discrimination and ostracism from other people, if they knew about it."

Still Danny didn't say anything, so Michael continued, unloading his concerns before he lost his nerve. "I'm sure I don't need to tell you about the dangers of AIDS." Michael's voice trembled slightly. He cleared his throat. "I'm not trying to hurt your feelings, Danny. I'm telling you this because I love you."

Danny chewed his lip and stared at a spot on the rug.

When he didn't answer, Michael continued, "If you think it would do any good, why don't you go see a counselor there and try to get some help. You can have him send the bill to me."

Danny straightened up and took a deep breath. "Sure, Dad. By the way, it looks like I'll have to stay here this summer and take a class in order to graduate. Maybe I can come home for a few weeks before fall quarter starts."

"Oh. That's too bad, Danny," Michael said in disappointment. "I was hoping you could be home this summer. It's been a long time since I've spent any time with you or even seen you. But I guess the most important thing right now is to plan for graduation."

He cleared his throat again. "Well, take care, and good luck on your finals. Goodbye, Danny."

" 'Bye, Dad."

If anyone had been able to see both Michael and Danny as they hung up, they would have been struck by the identical way they stood for a moment, staring pensively at the phone, then straightened their shoulders with a sigh and returned to their former pursuits.

In about a week, the first bill arrived from Dr. Slater, a psychotherapist practicing near the college. Kate picked up the mail.

"What's this?" She scrutinized the unfamiliar address. Tearing it open, she looked at the bill in surprise. "It looks like Danny went to see a therapist," she said apprehensively, handing it to Michael.

He glanced at the envelope with a grimace. "I told him to," he said flatly. "All I can say is, it had better get him over this nonsense." Kate was silent.

The next evening, Michael had to stay late at the office for a committee meeting. Kate paced restlessly around the house. Almost without thinking, she picked up the phone and dialed Danny's room.

"Hi, buddy," she greeted him. "We got a bill from Dr. Slater yesterday. I'm surprised that Daddy suggested you go and see him, knowing how he feels about psychiatrists, but I'm glad he did. Did it help to talk to him?"

"Yeah, it really did. Actually, I had gone to see him once before Dad called, and I paid for it myself. He said I should probably come back for two or three more sessions, at least."

"Well, I think you should go if it's helping. What . . . what does he tell you?" Kate asked, curious, but trying not to probe.

"Oh, mostly he just encourages me to talk about how I feel. He's trying to help me accept myself."

"Oh," murmured Kate. Somehow, that wasn't quite what she had expected to hear. She realized she had been hoping Dr. Slater would help Danny to change, would "cure" him, but that didn't seem to be his goal.

Feeling suddenly tired, Kate sank down on the bed and leaned back against the pillows. She didn't want to discourage Danny from getting help, but she wasn't sure this was the kind of help he needed. Uncomfortable, she abruptly changed the subject. "Are your exams all over?"

"Yeah. I think I passed 'em all. I have a two-week break before summer school. I'm going to be working full time in the student affairs office next week, and the following week I'm going up to Portland."

"Portland!" exclaimed Kate. "Why are you going up there?"

"Have you ever heard of Kinship?" Danny asked.

"No, I don't think so."

"It's a kind of support group for gays in the church, and they're having a camp meeting just outside Portland."

Kate was nonplussed. "Well, that's nice," she said at last.

The church has a support group for gays? "Do they have speakers and all?" she asked, puzzled.

"Well, as I understand it, they're not officially recognized by the church," Danny explained, "but some ministers from the church come and speak for some of the meetings."

After she said goodbye, Kate was surprised to find herself feeling almost jealous of Danny. What a relief it would be to talk to somebody. If she could find someone sympathetic, someone who was nonjudgmental, someone she could feel safe with . . . Maybe Michael would be willing for her to go talk to a therapist herself.

But when the second bill came, Michael frowned. "How long is this going to go on?" he muttered. Kate looked at him with a worried expression.

When she saw a third bill in the stack of mail, Kate braced herself for an explosion.

"This is ridiculous!" Michael fumed. "It just doesn't make any sense to pay somebody good money to listen to you talk!"

"But, honey, Danny says it's helping him!"

"Helping! How?" Michael exclaimed. "He still thinks he's a homosexual, doesn't he? I'm going to call Danny and tell him to stop."

"But . . ." Kate started to answer, then clamped her mouth shut. She knew how Michael felt about psychiatrists. But she wondered how this would make Danny feel, since Michael had suggested it in the first place.

The next time she talked to Danny, she was relieved when he said, "Well, I was beginning to feel guilty about you paying those bills anyway, because I knew Dad was expecting him to change me." Still, Kate wished Danny could have gotten more help.

A few weeks later, with the bright sunlight of a summer Sabbath morning bathing the sanctuary in stained-glass peace, Kate stood beside Michael and felt her heart soar as the pipe organ filled the church with the glorious strains of the morning hymn. "O Zion, haste; thy mission high fulfilling," she sang in her gentle alto. As she began the third verse, her voice faltered, and quick tears filled her eyes.

"Give of thy sons to bear the message glorious." *Danny . . . Oh, Danny!* Danny was studying to be a teacher. He had dreamed of returning to Singapore to teach in the mission school someday. She and Michael had been so happy that their son wanted to serve God as they did. But now . . . Through the rest of the hymn, Kate fought to control her tears, silently willing Michael not to notice.

The turmoil of her thoughts separated Kate from the service, until she heard the minister say, "God is waiting for you, for me, to face up to our pain and brokenness so He can demonstrate His power to renew our lives. He is waiting for us to bring our pain and pour it out at the cross. Only when we have surrendered it to Him can He use it to transform our self-centered lives into channels for His love."

Oh, thought Kate with an inner gasp of recognition, *I certainly have become aware of the pain and brokenness in my life. Are You trying to get my attention, God?*

Bill, the youth pastor, stood at the door as Kate and Michael were leaving the sanctuary. "God bless you, Kate! Michael!" he greeted them and shook hands firmly. *Did I imagine a searching look?* Kate wondered.

Danny seemed to be quite close to Bill, she remembered. *He asked me to invite Bill and his wife over for dinner one weekend when he and Angela were home, and I remember him talking to Bill a number of times after church.*

Maybe Bill knows about Danny, Kate speculated. The more she thought about it, the more sure she was. *Would I dare talk to Bill?* she wondered. She remembered Dr. Zimmerman's recommendation. Her need to talk to someone was very great. Since her one conversation with Michael, he had tried to avoid the topic of Danny's homosexuality.

But can I admit to Bill that one of our children has such a problem? Kate cringed. *After all, Michael and I are both leaders in this church, as well as in the denomination. We're supposed to be examples, to help other members with their problems, not to have problems ourselves.*

But after several days, Kate's desperate need to talk to

somebody won out over her sense of shame, and she rang the church office and asked for an appointment.

Bill welcomed her into his comfortable office, lined with bookshelves. Nervously, she sat down on the chair across from his desk. Coming straight to the point, she asked, "Bill, do you know about Danny?" After a pause, she clarified, "That he's homosexual?"

"Yes, Danny has talked to me a couple of times about it," Bill answered gently.

Kate folded and unfolded a tissue. With difficulty, she asked the question closest to her heart. "Is Danny going to be lost?"

Bill leaned forward intently and picked up a pen, rolling it between his fingers. "Kate, Danny didn't choose to have a homosexual orientation," he answered. "The feelings that he has are not sinful in themselves; it's what he does about those feelings that's important. Anyone who is single, whether heterosexual or homosexual, must struggle with controlling his or her sexual desires; even married people can have temptations. But it is only when we nurture immoral thoughts and act on them that they become sin."

Kate silently mulled over his words. At last, she responded wistfully, "If only he and Angela had gotten married, maybe he could have overcome this."

Bill shook his head. "Kate, I think Danny did the honorable thing by breaking his engagement to Angela when he realized that he couldn't love her in the same way she loved him. Sometimes homosexual men get married, thinking it will help them overcome their orientation, but it doesn't work that way. Instead, they often bring heartache to their wives, their children, and themselves, because their secret eventually becomes known. There is an example of that situation right here in our church."

"You mean Jay," Kate said, startled. Why hadn't she thought of him before? Jay and Sheila were neighbors and good friends. Although it had happened before she and Michael moved to the area, Kate had heard the story. Jay had been a popular and well-liked principal of the local church high school, until he was seen leaving a gay bar. Remorseful and repentant, he had admitted his homosexuality and agreed to enter counseling.

Instead of running away from the scene of their disgrace, Jay and Sheila had chosen to stay and live it down. Both Kate and Michael admired their courage and, as they became better acquainted, had almost forgotten their background. In fact, in the months since finding out about Danny, Kate had not even thought of Jay's situation in connection with him. Jay was active in the church, and his warmth and creativity made him an effective personal ministries leader. But Kate realized Bill was right. Jay and Sheila had certainly known heartache. Maybe . . .

"Bill, do you think Jay has become . . . heterosexual?" Kate asked.

Bill sighed. "No, Kate. But he has made an educated choice. He has chosen his family—his wife and children—over his sexual desires. Make no mistake; that is not an easy decision. But I believe God has honored and blessed him because of it."

Kate looked thoughtfully out the window, then turned back to Bill. Another question plagued her. "Bill, this has been so painful for Danny—for all of us—I just can't understand . . ."

She started over, in a more direct way. "Danny told me he prayed every day for years that God would change him and make him like other boys. If he wanted so much to be normal, why couldn't God have changed him?"

Bill was silent for a moment as he toyed with his pen. At last, he looked up with a sigh. "This is something no one really understands very well, Kate. I think maybe it is just something he will have to live with."

Suddenly, the possibility of a situation she had not really considered before loomed in Kate's mind. "What will I do if Danny finds a lover?" she wailed.

Bill stiffened. He hesitated, then said, "If it were my child, I would treat him the same way I would if he were on drugs. I'd say, 'I love you, but if you are going to take drugs, you can't live in my house.' If my son were gay and had a lover, I would let him know that he was not welcome to bring that person into my home."

Kate could understand Bill saying that, but in part of her mind, a newly acquired sensitivity made her aware of how those words could hurt. *How can that attitude be reconciled with the idea of unconditional love?* she wondered. Somehow, Bill's words conveyed a feeling of disgust and repulsion. Kate sensed that he didn't have real sympathy or understanding for the struggles a homosexual person faced.

"Bill . . . is it my fault, . . . or Michael's, that Danny is a homosexual? I've heard that if a boy is too close to his mother or isn't close enough to his father, that may cause him to be homosexual. I . . . I . . . I don't think our relationship is unhealthy. . ."

To her consternation, Kate's voice was shaking uncontrollably, and the tears that were always close to the surface these days streamed down her cheeks. Her tissue was in shreds, and Bill pushed a box across the desk for her.

Kate continued doggedly, "It's just that Danny and I have always had so much in common—music, writing, art—that we have been very close, but I never saw anything wrong with it. And, of course, Michael is very busy and engrossed with his work, much more so now than when Alex and Brenden were growing up, and he really hasn't had much time to do things with Danny, although I know he loves him. But he never has really seemed to understand Danny very well . . ." Her voice trailed off, and her shoulders began shaking with sobs.

"Kate, you and Michael mustn't blame yourselves," Bill said firmly. "As parents, we do the best we can, but we're human, and we make mistakes, all of us. And nobody really knows for sure what causes homosexuality. I don't think the things you mentioned are the reason Danny is homosexual, but even if they were, you have to remember that God understands. He works with us where we are right now, and He can bring something good out of the most hopeless-looking situations."

Kate struggled to regain her composure as she thanked Bill and said goodbye. Leaving his office, she slipped into the restroom across the hall and bathed her eyes with cold water before heading back to work.

An hour later, Kate's fingers were flying over the keyboard as she finished making corrections on a manual she was updating. She stopped to spell-check her document before printing it out. At that moment, her phone rang. It was Sheila, who worked in an office upstairs.

"Hi, Kate. Jay just called and said he needs to work late tonight," she said with a sigh. "Do you think I could catch a ride home with you and Michael?"

"Sure," Kate answered. "See you at the front entrance at 5:30."

After hanging up, Kate stared thoughtfully at the phone. *I wonder if Jay would be willing to talk to Danny?* she mused.

As she and Sheila chatted on the way home that evening, Kate couldn't put the thought out of her mind. But how could she arrange it? She didn't want to embarrass Jay or Sheila. She couldn't come up with a solution to the problem, but the idea stayed in the back of her mind.

After dropping Sheila off, Kate and Michael pulled up in front of their house. "What's for supper?" Michael asked, opening the car door for his wife.

For a moment, Kate sat motionless with her eyes closed, feeling as if a heavy weight were pressing her against the seat. The constant tug-of-war with her emotions was exhausting. Drawing a deep breath, she slowly pushed herself to her feet.

"I don't know," she answered listlessly. "I'm too tired even to think about it."

Michael put his arm around her shoulders and drew her close as they turned up the walk. "What's the matter, hon?" he asked sympathetically.

Kate let her head fall against his shoulder for a moment but ignored his question. As they reached the door, she squared her shoulders and sighed. "I think there's still some lentil soup left. And I guess I could make toasted lettuce-and-tomato sandwiches."

"Sounds good," Michael said cheerfully as he gave her a playful spank and strode into the family room to turn on the TV.

After supper was over, Kate loaded the dishwasher automatically, her thoughts going over her conversation with Bill that afternoon and her idea of getting Jay to talk to Danny. It seemed as if all she ever thought about anymore was Danny's problem.

Absentmindedly, she cut a slice of bread and dropped it into the toaster. She wasn't hungry; in fact, she felt full; yet there still seemed to be a huge empty place inside. When the toast popped up, she spread it with butter and drizzled honey over it. Standing over the sink as she ate, she suddenly wondered why she was eating again. Disgusted, she rinsed her fingers and tore off a paper towel, wiping toast crumbs from her lips.

She walked into the family room and stood behind Michael's chair, intending to tell him that she was going to bed early. Ruffling his hair with one hand, her attention was caught by the documentary that was just beginning, following the evening news. A father and mother hovered over a young woman on a hospital bed; then a photo of two women smiling at the camera with their arms around each other filled the screen.

"She is my lover," said a woman's voice. "Now that she cannot care for herself, I want to take care of her." Kate half expected Michael to switch to another channel. When he didn't, she sat down on the couch instead of saying goodnight.

As the story unfolded, Kate and Michael sat silently staring at the screen, absorbed in their own thoughts and reactions. It was the story of two women, lesbians, who had lived together for eighteen years, when one of them was in an automobile accident that left her in a coma. Ignoring the longtime bond between the two women, the parents of the injured one had immediately taken control of her life and care, refusing to allow her partner to have anything more to do with her.

As she watched, Kate felt torn by conflicting emotions. Her moral beliefs told her that it was not God's will for two women to live together as lovers. Yet she could not help seeing the deep love, as well as the hurt and grief, of the woman from whose life a companion of many years had been torn. She could not simply sit back, detached from the situation, in self-righteous judgment and condemnation, as she once would have. Now, because of her knowledge of Danny's situation, she was projected right into the middle of the tragic predicament faced by the woman in the story.

She found her sympathies marshaling around her, rather than around the parents who were determined to do everything possible to keep her away from their daughter. The pain of the woman on TV became her pain, and Kate felt hot tears sliding down her cheeks. Even when she felt Michael looking at her, she could not stop crying.

At last, in a voice that echoed her own pain, Michael exclaimed in frustration, "This is killing you, Kate!" In that moment, in spite of all that remained unspoken between them, Kate suddenly realized that Michael had been much more aware of her suffering than she had thought. *And maybe*, it occurred to her, *he also thinks about Danny's situation more than he lets on.* Still, she sensed his reluctance to talk to her about it.

When the program was over, Kate got slowly to her feet. She was surprised when Michael spoke. "Gives you a little different perspective, doesn't it?" he commented reflectively. "But, Kate . . . ," he looked up at her pleadingly. "You just can't let this tear you up so. It's going to kill you!"

Tears overflowed again, and Kate couldn't speak past the lump in her throat, but she leaned over and gently kissed his forehead in an attempt to give—and find—comfort.

As Danny passed the bank of mailboxes in the lobby of his dorm, he glanced quickly at the slot numbered 446. Surprised to see the white envelope, he checked his course and retrieved it. A feeling of warm anticipation stole over him as he saw his father's distinctive handwriting. A letter from his dad was rare enough to be considered a special occasion, although at this point in his life, he wasn't sure just what to expect.

He waited until he reached the privacy of his own room before tearing it open. As he read, a mask of pain spread over his features, and tears filled his eyes, to be replaced by a certain look of hardness and determination.

Grimly, Danny strode out of his room, slamming the door behind him, and headed for the campus computer center. He was glad to find it deserted as he sat down and began to vent his hurt feelings somewhat incoherently in a long letter to his parents.

Dear Dad and Mom,

I love you. Know that forever.

But I'm really quite terribly tired of being afraid, of letting my fear of breaking your hearts hang over my head. I've put off dealing with you because I haven't wanted to have to face that fear. Well, tonight, I got tired of being afraid. I felt furious with myself for letting this fear go on. I hate myself for not loving myself!

I can't change you. I can't make you understand me. I can only change what goes on in my own head, especially how I react to other people. God made us all independent beings, who think unique thoughts and have unique personalities, and we can either accept each other or not.

Dad, some of the things you have said and written have really hurt. And the reason I am writing is that they have hurt too much. I have opened myself up to you, and it is too painful to have you come back and tell me that I am lost, that I will lose most of my friends, that I will die young, that I will send my mother to an early grave. I cannot live with that degree of pain.

I didn't choose this life for myself, but even so, I have to find my own peace, my own path. This is MY life! Because I care deeply about how you feel and what you think, I have listened and will continue to listen to what you say. But I cannot, for my own sake, allow you to continue to wound me.

I know we'll all three blunder. Mom and Dad, I won't cut you off the first time you make a mistake. I won't cut you off. Period. I just have to set certain boundaries. Good fences make good neighbors, they say, and it's true enough. At times, you have to define your boundaries and make it clear just what point is too far for someone else to intrude.

I know you aren't being spiteful or trying to hurt me. Nor do I have any wish to hurt you. You love me. I love you. We want to keep communicating. We'll have to get used to new corners, new definitions, new boundaries to our relationships, but I know we can do it. It'll just take time on all our parts.

I love you. Know that forever.
Danny

The choir was already singing warm-up exercises when Kate hurried into the choir room. "Ah-ah-ah-ah-ah, Oo-oo-oo-oo-oo," she joined them as she slipped her arms into the flowing sleeves of her purple choir robe. She pulled the ivory satin stole over her head, centering the point, and picked up her music folder before finding her seat at the end of the back row.

"Take out the anthem," said Don, the choir director. "Sopranos, keep it light and floating on that first phrase." It was one of Kate's favorite pieces, "For the Beauty of the Earth," set to music by John Rutter. They had only gone through the piece once when Don glanced at the clock.

"Time to go. Let's pray."

After prayer, Kate led the way into the choir loft. Don seated the choir, then took his place at the organ. As she listened to the prelude, Kate glanced out over the church, crowded with worshipers. Her eyes lifted to the breathtaking stained-glass window that dominated the back wall of the sanctuary. She studied the magnificent mosaic of luminous glass pieces, in varying intensities of purple, blue, and scarlet, separated by black leading. Somehow, it reminded her of a quilt.

The prelude finished, the choir stood to sing the introit. Kate's heart felt high and lifted up as their blended voices raised in a glorious invocation of God's presence. Throughout the first part of the service, she was caught up in the experience of worship. But after the pastor entered the pulpit and began his sermon, her exaltation slowly faded, and all the old distress and worries over Danny assailed her once again.

It was in church that her emotions seemed to be the most vulnerable. In every sermon that Dave preached, God seemed to be speaking directly to her. This morning he was talking about how parents feel such a heavy responsibility for their children's salvation.

Then Kate heard him say something that really struck home. "But that's really not your responsibility," he stated. "Your job is just to love them; it's God's job to save them."

As so often happened these days, Kate could not control the tears that sprang to her eyes. She stared straight ahead as the gorgeous colors of the stained-glass window swam and blurred.

Yes, God, she thought, *only You can save Danny. But I can show him how much I love him, and maybe that will be a reminder of Your love.* During the rest of the church service, she mulled that thought over in her mind.

As the organ thundered out the introduction to the final hymn and choir and congregation stood to sing, Kate suddenly had a vision. She would make Danny another quilt, a quilt as beautiful as the stained-glass window, a quilt as beautiful as she knew his life could still be.

Chapter 7

A Heartache Shared

It was nine o'clock on a warm July evening. Michael, who had just finished watering the lawn, was cooling off with a glass of lemonade in the kitchen. Kate was at the piano playing "Clair de Lune," when the doorbell chimed.

"Who could that be at this hour?" Kate exclaimed, as Debussy was abruptly interrupted. She crossed the room and opened the door.

"Laura! Greg!" she exclaimed in surprise. "Come on in. To what do we owe the honor of your company?"

Greg offered a lame excuse as he followed his wife in the door. Michael came in from the kitchen. "Hey, Greg and Laura! Long time, no see!" he exclaimed.

Greg dropped down onto one corner of the couch while Laura perched on the edge of her seat beside him. Michael headed for his favorite wingback chair and lowered himself into it with a tired sigh. Kate sat down on the piano bench, facing them, with one leg tucked under her.

After a few moments of general conversation, Greg came to the point. "Well, actually, we're here tonight because of your son," he said, looking at the floor. Questions flashed through Kate's mind.

"Which son?" Michael asked cautiously. Something in Greg's eyes made him add, "Danny?"

Greg nodded in confirmation. Kate felt her stomach lurch.

"Shelly called us tonight," Greg said. "She told us she had seen Danny at Kinship Kamp Meeting, and she thought you

65

might need us. You do know what Kinship is, don't you?"

The blood had drained from Kate's face. "Yes," she said slowly. "It's a kind of support group for homosexuals in the church. But does Shelly . . . , is Shelly . . ."

"Shelly is lesbian," Laura finished softly.

"Oh, Laura!" Kate wailed in dismay.

It was almost as much a shock as finding out about Danny. Greg and Laura were good friends, and their daughter Shelly, a few years older than Danny, was a special young woman. Bright and talented, she was a research chemist with a large pharmaceutical company.

Laura crossed the room quickly and knelt beside Kate. "I know how you feel," she whispered as she put her arm around Kate's shoulder. As their tears flowed, Michael and Greg stared at them in painful silence.

After a few minutes, Kate regained her composure. "How long have you known?" she asked, wiping her tears away.

"We found out three years ago," Laura said, giving Kate's shoulder a squeeze as she stood up and went back to the couch. "Shelly spent a year as a student missionary in Indonesia, you know, and Greg visited her there on his way to Australia. She told him then." She looked over at Greg.

Greg leaned forward with his elbows on his knees. "She had been hoping her year there would help her sort out her feelings and get them under control," he said, staring at his hands, "but instead, she finally had to face the fact that she was a lesbian and couldn't change. She was really upset, almost suicidal, when she told me about it. It helped her when I took the news quite calmly and she realized I wasn't going to reject her."

Kate could hardly take it in. It seemed unbelievable that someone they knew as well as Greg and Laura could have hidden their heartache so successfully. But perhaps that explained Laura's bouts with neuralgia, she realized. And then there was the time Greg had given her a ride to work. He had told her all about some research with rats that showed when they were stressed at a certain stage during their pregnancy, all their offspring exhibited homosexual behavior. She had been a little surprised at his interest in the subject, but now she understood.

Kate's thoughts returned to the present as Laura continued Shelly's story. "Shelly told us later that she had wondered why she never felt the way other girls did about boys, but it wasn't until her senior year in high school that she discovered her attraction to girls. One day, her best friend came to her in tears because her boyfriend had broken up with her. Shelly said that as she put her arms around her to comfort her, she suddenly realized this was what she had always been looking for."

Laura paused. Kate could see that even after several years, her friend still found the memory painful. "Shelly said it felt so right and so good to hold a girl in her arms; she had never felt that way with any of the boys she had dated. She was so upset by this discovery that she ran out of the room and wandered around in the rain, crying, for hours."

"Oh, poor Shelly," Kate murmured sympathetically.

Still finding the whole thing hard to believe, she asked, "Did Danny and Shelly know about each other before?"

A faint smile crossed Laura's face. "No, I guess they gave each other quite a shock," she answered dryly. "Shelly said she was standing in line at the cafeteria that first evening when she looked back and saw Danny some distance behind her. At the same moment, he looked up and saw her."

Laura gave a little chuckle, remembering Shelly's description. "She said they both screeched in surprise and went running toward each other, babbling in amazement! They kept asking, 'Are you . . . ? Are you really . . . ? Are you gay too?' "

Kate smiled briefly as she pictured the scene, then her face grew serious again. "I don't understand about Kinship," she said, looking questioningly from Laura to Greg. "Danny says it's not recognized by the church."

Greg leaned back and stretched his legs out in front of him. "That's right," he answered, raising an eyebrow and staring at the pillow he had picked up from the couch.

"The people in Kinship want to be a part of the church, but they don't agree with the traditional interpretation of biblical texts that refer to homosexuality," he explained. "They believe the Bible condemns homosexual acts if they are engaged in by people who are heterosexual, but they believe that for them, this is normal behavior. Of course, the church doesn't accept that interpretation."

Kate looked troubled. "No, of course not," she agreed.

There was a moment of silence before Laura spoke. "But Kinship does offer understanding and sympathy that homosexuals don't find anywhere in the church; I think that's why it has such appeal. They need somewhere to turn for help, and the church has pretty much ignored their problem."

Kate nodded in agreement, remembering the feelings of alienation Danny had expressed. "What's happened with Shelly since she first told you?" she asked.

Laura sighed. "She has become quite involved with Kinship. And . . . , she lives with Jonna, her . . . well, they have what they call a committed relationship. In fact, they even had a special ceremony, committing themselves to each other."

A stirring from Michael's corner caused Kate, Greg, and Laura to turn and look at him, as if they had each suddenly noticed his absence from their conversation.

Michael's jaw set more firmly, as it always did when he was uncomfortable with something. He picked up his glass and sipped slowly before asking, "How do you feel about that?"

"Well, we don't like it, of course," Greg answered. "We don't think that it's God plan for their lives. But we want Shelly to know we will always love her, even if we believe she has made a wrong choice. After all, we don't always make the right choices, either, and God hasn't stopped loving us."

Kate nodded. "That's how I feel about Danny too."

Michael cleared his throat. "I'm not totally convinced that Danny is really homosexual," he said with a frown. "I think it's pretty normal for young men to go through a phase of unsettled sexual feelings in their teens. Danny is just so sensitive I think maybe he has talked himself into thinking those feelings mean he's gay."

Kate shook her head in frustration. Michael just couldn't

seem to admit there was a real problem. "But, honey, Danny said he prayed for years that God would change him," she reminded him. "He said he dated girls in high school, trying to feel the way other boys felt. I don't think that sounds like he was talking himself into thinking he was gay."

Michael's expression suddenly turned bleak. "Well, I hope he comes to his senses before he ruins his life," he said.

"It's a hard thing to come to terms with," agreed Laura, with a sympathetic glance at Michael. "I'm sure Danny appreciates your love and concern. A lot of parents reject their children when they find out."

"That's right," Greg agreed. "It wasn't easy for us when Shelly told us. I think it was harder for Laura than for me." He looked over at Laura, and she nodded. "But we're glad now that we didn't let it ruin our relationship with Shelly."

Greg ran his finger along the piping on the pillow he was holding. "You know who Moira Cox is, don't you?" he asked suddenly. "She goes to our church."

"You mean that older woman with the accent, who wears her hair pulled back in a bun?" Kate asked.

"Yes, the one who usually sits near the front on the left," Greg replied. "She's such a meek, quiet sort of person that this is hard to believe, but a couple of years ago, her son who lived out in Seattle called to tell her that he was gay and dying of AIDS. She apparently felt that she had to express her disapproval of his lifestyle by refusing his phone calls and returning his letters and packages. She never spoke or wrote to him again. He died a few months later."

"Oh, how terrible!" Kate exclaimed. "She must surely be sorry now that she let him die like that!"

"I suppose so," Greg agreed, nodding his head sadly. "But so many parents seem to feel that it's their duty to express strong disapproval when their child chooses a sinful lifestyle. I think they're afraid that if they continue to show their love, they will be seen as encouraging or condoning the sinful behavior. They forget that the Bible says God loved us while we were still sinners."

"I'm sure part of the problem is the misunderstanding

most people have about homosexuality," Laura observed, taking off her glasses and massaging the bridge of her nose. "They think it's a choice that people make. But I was talking to Dr. Martin, and he told me that some of the latest research suggests that homosexual orientation has a genetic basis."

Michael pulled one leg up across his other knee and drew his lips into a straight line. "If a person has no control over being homosexual, then why does the Bible say it is a sin?"

"I think that the *condition* of being homosexual is a *result* of sin in the world," Greg said thoughtfully. "We know that God did not create people as homosexuals in the beginning, and I don't believe homosexuality was ever part of His plan. But because of generations of sinful behavior, people today may not be able to help having a homosexual orientation. However, they can, with God's help, choose not to live that lifestyle. I think that's where sin comes in."

The lamplight made shadows on Laura's face as she said softly, "I'm sure it's not easy for our kids. Shelly has helped us see that your sexual orientation is so much more than just the act of having sex with someone. It's an integral part of your personality and affects everything you do and think."

Tears welled up in Kate's eyes as she tried to imagine the enormity of what Danny and Shelly had to contend with. "Then, maybe . . . , maybe, you could say that those feelings of . . . attraction, which just come to them naturally, are not a sin unless they act on them. I mean, teenagers—boys and girls—certainly have strong feelings of attraction for each other, but we don't consider that a sin unless they let those feelings control them and lead them to having sex outside of marriage. And for a boy or girl who just naturally feels attracted to someone of the same sex, it seems to me we would have to look at it the same way, wouldn't we?"

Greg and Laura nodded in agreement. "I don't think God holds people responsible for feelings over which they have no control, any more than He holds someone responsible for being born blind or handicapped in some other way," Greg said softly.

But Michael shook his head. "God asks the same thing of homosexuals that He asks of unmarried heterosexuals—sexual purity. Abstinence. We don't think that's too much to ask of them; why should it be so much worse for homosexuals?"

Kate spoke up quickly, without stopping to weigh her answer. "It seems sad to me, because unmarried heterosexuals can at least look forward to the hope of finding someone to love and marry someday. But homosexuals, if they believe that God forbids homosexual acts, know they can never hope to have that kind of relationship. I know that's no excuse, but it means they have to lead a very lonely life. They can't even have a roommate to share their lives with."

"Another thing that I think makes a homosexual's situation more difficult to bear is the stigma he or she feels," Greg said. "Not just the church, but society as a whole, has an irrational hatred and fear of homosexuals. There is still so much ignorance and misunderstanding about the subject."

Greg looked at his watch. "Nearly eleven o'clock!" he exclaimed. "We've got to go home! But before we leave, let's ask God to be with our children and to show us how we can help them."

As they knelt, Kate thought what a comfort it was to have someone who could share their sorrow and understand what they were going through.

Near the end of July, Michael left on another trip. This time he would be gone for nearly three weeks while visiting several islands in the Caribbean. After he had gone, the long summer evenings stretched out emptily ahead of Kate.

One afternoon, on her way home from work, she stopped at her favorite fruit stand. A table heaped with watermelons caught her eye. She thumped several until she found one that sounded just right and carried it to the cashier.

At home, she sank a long knife into its center, and it split open with a satisfying crack. "Ah, perfect!" she murmured. Carrying a big quarter piece of melon on a tray, she went out to sit at the picnic table in the backyard.

She could feel herself beginning to relax in the languorous late-afternoon heat. As she swallowed sweet, juicy bites of red watermelon, she gazed reflectively into the leafy green depths overhead. A mockingbird burst into brief song from its hidden perch somewhere above.

When the melon was finished clear down to the rind, Kate pushed it aside and rested her head on her arms, enjoying a rare moment of idleness. At last, she stood up and carried her tray back to the house. *I think I'll bring my quilt pieces out and sew till it gets dark*, she decided.

The phone was ringing as she opened the door, and she hurried to answer it. Laura was calling.

"Brace yourself, Kate," Laura said gently. "I think I mentioned to you that Kinship publishes a newsletter. We have a subscription to it, and the latest issue came today.

"Kate . . . , Danny wrote the article that's headlined on the front page. He used his own name. A lot of people who write for the newsletter use pseudonyms, but Danny didn't. He's a very courageous boy, Kate, and I know he doesn't want to hide and pretend to be something he's not. But I thought you'd want to know. It could make things harder for you."

Kate felt a hot flush sweep over her face. "Who . . . who might see it?" she asked uncertainly.

"I'm not sure," Laura answered carefully. "But I think probably there are several administrators at the church headquarters who get copies."

"And Danny's article is on the front page, you say?" Kate asked with a sinking heart.

"Yes, it's a report on his experiences at Kamp Meeting. It's very well done, Kate. Danny's a talented writer. Would you like to see my copy?"

"I think so," Kate said slowly. "But, Laura, what do you think will happen when people see Danny's article?"

"Probably nothing," Laura assured her quickly. "I really don't think anybody will say or do anything about it. In fact, so many publications cross their desks, they may just give it a quick glance and not even notice his name. I just didn't want you to be unpleasantly surprised. Try not to worry about it, Kate."

"Easier said than done." Kate sighed. "When can I see the newsletter?"

"I'll put it in your mailbox when I drive by tomorrow."

When Kate saw the manila envelope with Laura's return address, she opened it with a sense of dread. There was Danny's name, big as life, on the front page, but as she read the article, she was caught up in his reactions to his first meeting with a group of people like himself and the poignancy of his sense of self-discovery. Even though she still cringed at the possibility of people she knew reading it, Kate was proud of the openness and vulnerability with which Danny described his emotions.

Danny's summer class would be over in a couple of weeks, and he would be coming home for a short vacation. As always, Kate looked forward to seeing him again. But this time she was fully aware that there would be no quick, easy solution to what she thought of as his "problem." It was something that would unalterably impact and change each of them for the rest of their lives.

As the day of Danny's arrival drew near, Kate's thoughts turned often to her idea of getting Jay to talk to him. *Surely,* she thought, *it would help Danny to talk with someone who can understand what he is going through. Jay could offer him advice based on his own experience.*

As she tried to think of a graceful way to arrange it, she remembered hearing that Jay and Dave, the senior pastor of their church, had been college classmates. Since Jay had transferred to their church after leaving his career as a high-school principal, Kate felt fairly certain that Dave must have been supportive as Jay and Sheila had put their lives back together. Maybe she could ask Dave to talk to Jay and see if he would feel comfortable about talking to Danny.

But that meant telling Dave about Danny, and it was still so terribly difficult to talk to anyone about it. Even though Dave was warm and friendly and easy to talk to, she hated the idea of telling him about her problems. She felt such a sense of failure. If she looked at her feelings closely, she realized they were probably motivated by pride, but she managed to convince herself that her reluctance to talk to Dave was because he was so busy and had to listen to so many people's problems.

Still, that seemed to be the only way to arrange a meeting between Jay and Danny, so at last, with much trepidation, she phoned Dave one morning. It was easier than she had thought it would be. Dave didn't act shocked. In fact, he told Kate that he had seen a copy of Kinship's newsletter at the home of one of his parishioners, so he already knew about Danny.

When Kate falteringly told him how hard it was, wondering what other people would think when they read it, Dave reassured her, "Kate, these people are your friends. They're not going to condemn you or Danny or stop loving you. I know they're just going to be praying for you and loving you all the more." He agreed to talk to Jay.

Since Danny had six weeks at home before the fall quarter started at college, he had applied for work at the church headquarters office. With his computer expertise and the speed and efficiency he had demonstrated during previous summer jobs, he easily found work in one of the offices.

One afternoon soon after Danny had come home, Kate had to leave the office early because of a dental appointment.

"No problem," Danny assured her. "I can probably catch a ride home with Sheila and Jay." Kate, who had not yet gotten around to broaching the subject of Jay and Danny meeting, agreed. Arriving home from the dentist's office a little earlier than she had expected, Kate was starting supper when she heard a car pull up in front. Glancing out the window, she saw it was Jay and Sheila's car.

Twenty minutes passed before Danny entered the house, looking thoughtful. "What were you talking about?" questioned Kate.

Danny hesitated before replying, "Jay was taking a vacation day and staying home with the girls, so it was just Sheila who brought me home. Somehow, we got to talking, and I told her about breaking up with Angela and why we broke up. Then she talked to me about what she and Jay have gone through."

Kate was amazed at how things had worked out. "What did she say?" she asked.

"She was really very open about it," Danny answered slowly. "She said Jay had told her when they were engaged that he was homosexual, but they both believed that getting married would take care of it. She told me her side of the story and what it has been like. I could see that it is still very painful for her to talk about. I really admire her and Jay for their courage and the effort they both have made to save their marriage."

Danny paused, then continued with a sigh, "Sheila told me she thought I had done the right thing to break up with Angela. And she said she would be praying for me."

A deep feeling of gratitude to Sheila for being willing to talk to Danny swept over Kate. "Danny," she ventured, "do you think it would help to talk to Jay too?"

Danny looked up, startled. "Yeah, I guess so," he said noncommittally.

"I've been thinking about that for quite a while," Kate confessed. "I didn't know how you'd feel about it, but I asked Dave to find out if Jay would be willing to talk to you. If it's OK with you, I'll check with him and see what he found out. I just thought that since Jay seems to have found some answers to his situation, he might be able to help you."

"Sure, I'd be willing to talk to him," Danny agreed, a little more positively.

Through Dave, Jay and Danny's meeting was set up for a few nights later at the church.

Satisfied that she had done what she could, Kate felt reticent about questioning Danny afterward. It was not until a couple of years later that Danny told her about their meeting.

"We told each other our stories," he said. "Jay admitted the trauma he and Sheila had been through, but he felt it was worth it to save his family. However, he said he believed that I had a right to choose how I wanted to live my life."

Chapter 8

It's Not Fair!

Kate parked her Honda in the shade of the old elm tree and turned to look at her dawn gray house framed by a pair of elegant blue spruce. A profusion of deep purple blooms covered the clematis vine that trailed across the porch.

With a sigh, she got out of the car, opened the mailbox, and retrieved a big bundle of mail. She carried it up the flagstone path and dropped into the white wicker rocking chair on the porch. Closing her eyes and gently pushing the rocker with her foot, Kate felt the day's tensions slowly drain away.

She was aware of a loud, pulsating *purr* a split second before a small, warm body landed in her lap with a plop. She looked down at the black cat stretching and purring ecstatically. "Oh, Beethoven, did you miss me?" she crooned, rubbing the hard little head.

After a bit, she put Beethoven down and went into the house. Michael was in California for a week, and the house was too quiet. As she turned on the radio, set to her favorite classical music station, the clean precision of a Bach fugue played on a guitar filled the kitchen. Kate sat down at the table to go through the mail. Preliminary sorting revealed a manila envelope covered with Danny's scrawling handwriting. Eagerly, she opened it.

Inside was a book and a folded sheet of paper. She glanced quickly at the book, *Annie on My Mind*, then opened the letter.

"Dear Mom," she read.

I know this letter is going to disappoint, and even hurt, you, but I don't want to have to hide things from you anymore.

For most of my life, I have felt different from other people—like I was on the outside, looking in. You can't possibly imagine how comforting and affirming it has been to become acquainted with some people who are like me. It was like meeting up with some long-lost relatives. I met them when I went to Kinship Kamp Meeting last June.

Mom, I feel such a sense of relief now that I have decided to be myself, free and honest. No more hiding and pretending to be something I'm not. I still want the same things I was hoping for with Angie. But Angie wasn't right for me. Someday I'm going to have a great relationship with someone. We'll wash dishes together, discuss a book on a car trip to the relatives, have our fights and resolve them, grouse at each other after a horrible day at work and laugh at ourselves afterward; we'll grow old together. After a long night of writing on a book, I want to climb into bed and lean my aching shoulders back with a sigh against his warm chest. We'll say "I love you" to each other and know we mean it past anything, through anything, forever . . .

And having said that, I'd like to tell you that, while I was at Kinship Kamp Meeting, I met someone who might become an important part of my life. His name is Mike Sheldon. He came up just for the weekend, and we immediately caught each other's eye. We sat together during vespers and took a walk afterward. We had quite a talk, and I hope you won't mind if I share some of it with you.

Mike told me he wasn't interested in casual affairs. "I'm a relationship kind of guy," he told me. "I like to take things slowly. I can live by myself if I have to. I just want to have a normal relationship with a person I can love and who will love and respect me and who wants to be committed."

I thought, *Hallelujah! He sounds like my kind of guy.* I know you'd like him, Mom. He's mature, wholesome, sensitive, romantic, sincere, honest, and knows where he's going.

At any rate, before Kamp Meeting was over, we agreed to write, and we've averaged about two letters and three or four phone calls a week since then. It's been an exciting time for both of us, and we've gotten to know each other very well, even though it has been long distance. I never realized how wonderful it could be getting to know someone at this level.

At this point, I don't know if we will end up establishing a permanent relationship or not, but this experience has confirmed my belief that a homosexual relationship is no different from a heterosexual one. There are the same misunderstandings, the same rapture, the same need for commitment, the same ordinary everydayness of it all! I'm planning to go up to Portland to see Mike next weekend, and maybe we will make a decision about our future.

Mom, I'll be honest. I feel very anxious about telling you this, but I want to be able to be open about the things that are important in my life. I'm interested in what you do, and I believe you're interested in my life too. Besides, you'd probably learn about it sooner or later, and I want to be the one to tell you. I don't have any illusions that you'll be thrilled! But then, although it would really be nice if you were able to get excited about such things with me, my true satisfaction and worth come from within; others' approval is just icing on the cake.

I know you're still hoping I can change, but I can't. God knows I've tried long enough. Read this

book, Mommy. I hope it will help you understand
me better. Your loving son,
Danny

Kate's eyes were blinded with tears before she got to the
end of the letter. She felt as if someone had just dealt her a
stunning blow, as if her last hope had just been snatched
away.

Until this moment, she had still cherished the hope that
Danny might be able to change, or at least would not choose
a gay lifestyle. Her mind rejected what he was saying, yet her
heart ached over his obvious yearning for understanding.
What a cruel dilemma he faced!

For a moment, anger flared in her heart. *How could God
allow someone so dear, someone with so much potential, to be
handicapped with such a terrible problem? It isn't fair!*

No, whispered another part of her mind, *none of the results
of sin are fair. But God is not the author of sin; it's Satan who
causes all the sorrow and misery in the world.*

But why doesn't God do something about it? her heart cried
out. *Think of the pain Danny has had to suffer all these years
alone, from the time he was just a little boy. And I didn't know
anything about it! I couldn't help him! Maybe I even made it
worse for him!*

With a pang, Kate recalled an evening a couple of years
earlier when Michael, Danny, and she had been sitting in the
family room watching the news on TV. One of the news
stories had been about a gay-rights parade on the Mall in
Washington, D.C. The camera had zoomed in close on two
young men walking with their arms around each other's
waists. Realizing they were on camera, they had kissed.

"Oh, gross!" Kate had exclaimed, aversion obvious in her
voice. Now, for the first time, it occurred to her how that must
have sounded to Danny. Although, at that point, he probably
had not even been close to choosing a gay lifestyle, he
couldn't help realizing that his mother had been repulsed by
people who were like him. And those young men on TV?
Looking back, she had to admit that they had been clean-cut,

nice-looking boys. Perhaps they hadn't been so different from Danny.

For long moments, Kate sat with her head bowed, lost in grief and despair. At last, she lifted her head and listlessly picked up the book Danny had sent, and another folded paper fell out. Opening it, she saw it was a poem.

I Long for Angela

Yet I would bend my tired forehead
to a man's shoulder,
feeling the press of his warm flesh
shaped and held by firm and gentle muscles,
and inhaling the strong comfort of his scent.

I would share them both
yet I have neither:

To remember Angela is to pain
her free joy,
winsome petulance;
she was innocent!
so dependent!

And to think on him is to ache.

I am sad with a resonance that all throbs my soul.

Kate burst into groaning sobs. Was there no end to the pain? She felt an overwhelming longing for comfort and sympathy in this wrenching sorrow, but to whom could she turn? Michael didn't want to talk about it. Greg and Laura were out of town. Her parents, on whom she had always counted for understanding, would also be devastated. A friend? She still shrank from revealing this to anyone. It was as if, since Danny had "come out of the closet," she had taken his place in it.

In an unconscious effort to deaden the pain, Kate took a box of crackers out of the cupboard and began munching as she moved around the kitchen, picking things up and putting them down aimlessly. Eventually she remembered that it was Wednesday evening, time for Midweek Manna, the small prayer-and-Bible-study group that she had recently joined.

She recoiled from the thought of facing anybody, but her need for some kind of human warmth was great, so she washed her face, brushed her salt-and-pepper hair, picked up her Bible, and walked out through the violet dusk to her car. A pale yellow harvest moon hung in the sky as she drove to church. Bruised and battered though she felt, a quiet peace stole into her heart as she looked at its serene beauty.

Hurrying into the committee room, she slipped quietly into a chair. Half a dozen women and two men were already seated around the long table. *How many of them are hiding an aching heart?* Kate wondered.

As if he had been waiting for her, Dave, the pastor, opened the meeting with prayer. They were studying the book of Mark, and Dave read the passage under discussion, verses 14 to 32 of chapter 9. It was the story of the man who had brought his son to the disciples to have his evil spirit cast out, only to find them unable to meet his need.

When Jesus appeared on the scene, the man turned to him and pleaded, " 'If you can do anything, take pity on us and help us.' "

" 'Everything is possible for him who believes,' " Jesus answered.

Sensing his need, the man cried out, " 'I do believe; help me overcome my unbelief.' "

Tears sprang to Kate's eyes as she echoed the man's words in her heart. Shielding her tear-filled eyes from view with her hand, she fixed her gaze on the Bible lying in front of her. *Lord, I can't imagine how You can bring anything good out of this situation, but I want to believe that You can,* she whispered in her heart. *Please help me with my lack of faith.* The discussion flowed around her, but she didn't take part, not trusting her voice.

"Are there any requests for prayer?" Dave asked at the end

of the discussion. Kate yearned to share her burden, but her voice seemed paralyzed.

After several others had spoken, Dave asked, "Any unspoken requests?" Thankfully, Kate raised her hand.

During prayer, Kate pulled a tissue out of her pocket, wiped her eyes, and blew her nose. When it was over, she closed her Bible and prepared to slip out quickly, but before she got to the door, she felt a hand on her arm.

"What's the matter, Kate?" Dave asked gently. Kate looked down as the others left, trying to keep from crying again.

At last, without looking up, she said softly, "I got a letter from Danny today. I've been hoping and praying that somehow God would change him or help him to live a celibate life, but his letter told me that he wants to spend his life with a man."

"Kate, we all make wrong choices from time to time," Dave said understandingly. "Danny is dealing with a very difficult situation. Maybe that's the only way out he can see right now. But no decision is final. He may have made the wrong choice this time, but God doesn't give up on him just because of that. God has a thousand ways of working with Danny that we can't even imagine. Let's keep on praying for him and trust God to be the 'Hound of Heaven,' staying on his trail as long as it takes to bring him back."

The thought warmed Kate's heart. "Thanks, Dave," she murmured gratefully. "I'm glad I came tonight; I almost didn't." Dave patted her shoulder encouragingly as she turned to go.

Back home, she picked up the book Danny had sent. What kind of book would it be? She felt reluctant to read it, but she was sure Danny had chosen it carefully, wanting to help them understand him. He was a thoughtful, sensitive boy; he wouldn't send them a book that would be offensive.

Slowly, she began reading. To her surprise, she found it was a story of two young women who became very close friends and eventually realized they were in love with each other. Somehow, that seemed easier to read about than if it had been two young men. It was a very sensitively written story, and the struggles the women went through in dealing with their feelings gave her some insight into what Danny might have experienced.

Even though she couldn't agree with the conclusion the book came to, which approved of the relationship, she could feel more understanding and sympathy for young men or women who felt the same kind of attraction for someone of their own sex that others would feel for someone of the opposite sex. Unless one were convinced that God had forbidden His children to have such relationships for their own good, only the conventions of society would be a deterrent. And even for someone like Danny, who had been raised to love and obey God, not being able to talk to anyone about his strong sexual feelings could lead to confusion and doubts.

It was 1:00 a.m. when Kate finished the book and turned off her lamp. Lying there in the darkness, exhausted from the emotions of the day, she turned Danny over to God and, for the first time in months, fell into a deep sleep.

Chapter 9

Prejudice

It was a cold, gloomy Friday in mid-November. Kate hurried home to her Friday-afternoon housecleaning chores. She grabbed the mail out of the box as she dashed to the house.

Ah! A letter from Danny! Even though they communicated regularly by phone, Danny still found time occasionally to write, and his letters were always special. Housecleaning temporarily forgotten, she dropped into a chair and tore the letter open.

Dear Mom and Dad,

It's 10:30 p.m., and I've been in the computer room working on some reading games for my third-grade students. Decided I might as well dash off a quick letter before I head back to the dorm for a few hours of sleep.

I'm enjoying my student teaching. Last night was the school talent show, and it was great! My roommate's sister, who is one of my reading students, did a cute recitation where she acted the part of a windup doll on a stand. The son of the English teacher I graded papers for last year recited a poem with about as much "uninhibition" as I've ever seen! A hilarious evening!

Next week my supervisor is going to videotape my class and then critique my teaching. The thought makes me a bit nervous.

You will probably be relieved to know that my

visit with Mike in Portland ended with us deciding that while we can be good friends, we aren't interested in establishing a long-term relationship.

I think I mentioned on the phone that I have gradually been letting some of my close friends in on the fact that I am gay. And so far everyone I've talked to has been very understanding and supportive. It is such a relief not to have to pretend to be something I'm not. Frankly, I think I have come to the place where I am ready to stop wearing my mask altogether. I just want to be honest about who I am, and if people can't accept that, then I don't need them. I even confided in one of the women I work with in the student affairs office, and she has just been great. She said anytime I needed someone to talk to, she's available. She is going to give me some books to read that she thinks will be helpful.

As Kate read, a worried frown wrinkled her forehead. Her worry was confirmed when Michael read the letter later.

"Danny's asking for trouble," he predicted grimly. "I'm afraid he's going to have some hard lessons to learn."

Kate was reminded of her worry a few days later. While eating lunch with friends at the cafeteria, the conversation turned to the previous day's news story about controversy over the government's funding of AIDS research.

"Why should the taxpayers have to pay for that research?" demanded one of the secretaries indignantly. "If those people would just change their lifestyle, there wouldn't be any need for AIDS research!"

"That's right!" agreed a man. "If they insist on continuing their perverted lifestyle, they deserve to die."

Kate cringed. Something in her cried out to challenge these harsh assessments, but she remained silent. Returning to her office, she berated herself for her cowardice. Remembering Michael's prediction, she trembled for Danny.

Kate left work early the last Wednesday of the month. She

mentally reviewed her Thanksgiving dinner menu as she wheeled her grocery cart up and down the aisles. Oranges, crushed pineapple, and coconut to make ambrosia. Celery, onions, and walnuts to go in the dressing. Potatoes and sweet potatoes, frozen peas, and a can of beets. Olives. And, of course, a can of pumpkin for the pie and whipped cream and toasted almonds to garnish it.

Brenden was teaching seventh and eighth grade in a church school in Virginia, and even though he was the only one who could make it home this year, Kate found herself in almost a festive mood. It seemed like such a long time since she had felt any sense of anticipation, any lifting of her spirits.

Smiling at the clerk, she paid for her groceries and hurried home. Michael, she found, already had a fire blazing in the family room and was engrossed in the evening newscast. Quickly and efficiently, she put the groceries away, then went to peer out the window. The sun was just setting, silhouetting black, leafless branches against the orange sky.

"I hope he gets here before dark," she murmured.

Michael looked up. "Are you worried?" he teased with a grin. "Well, he probably had to go home and pack after school was out. I doubt if he gets here before six."

"I bet he'll be starved," predicted Kate, going back to the kitchen to start supper. "I don't think he gets enough to eat."

She was stirring a kettle of tomato-rice soup when she heard Michael call out, "Here he is!"

Dropping her spoon, Kate flew to the door, where Michael already stood waiting. In the deepening dusk, she saw Brenden lifting his suitcase out of the trunk. He turned to wave. "Oh, Brenden, I'm so glad you're here!" she called. "How was your trip?"

"Lots of traffic on the beltway," he answered, closing his trunk and starting up the walk. "I'm kinda hungry. All I had for lunch was a burrito."

Kate grinned. "Supper's almost ready," she assured him. Brenden's arm went warmly around her shoulders as he stepped inside and shut the door against the brisk coldness of the evening air.

"Here, let me take your suitcase," offered Michael.

Brenden followed Kate to the kitchen. "How's Danny doing?" he asked.

It had only been a couple of weeks since Kate had told Brenden about Danny. When she had told Alex, she hadn't been surprised to learn that Danny had already confided in him. Although nine years apart, the two of them were alike in many ways. Alex had said simply, "I don't understand it, but he's my little brother, and I'll always love him."

But Kate hadn't been so sure how Brenden would react. Quieter than his brothers, he had always been the most dependable, as well as the easiest to discipline. He seemed to have a natural inclination to do what was right. She had wondered if he would be shocked. But when she told him, he had replied matter-of-factly. "Oh, really? Well, I'm not too surprised."

Now, in answer to Brenden's question, Kate said slowly, "I think he's all right. He says he's enjoying his student teaching. But I'm a little worried. Since he has come to terms with being homosexual, he seems to want to be so open about it. He says he's tired of hiding behind a mask."

"Yeah," Brenden said soberly. "I don't think he realizes how prejudiced some people are."

Kate nodded wordlessly, then drew a deep breath and smiled up at him. She wasn't going to let anything distract her from the joy of having Brenden home for Thanksgiving.

"Right now, let's get some supper into you," she commanded. "Get your hands washed, and sit down at the table."

"M-m-m! That soup smells good!" Brenden leaned over the pan of bubbling red liquid and sniffed deeply. "Hurry up! All of a sudden, I'm starved."

Kate brought a steaming spoonful of soup to her lips to taste. It was her special recipe, flavored with a little sour cream and peanut butter.

"It's ready," she announced. Sliding a tray of garlic-buttered French bread into the oven to toast, she ladled up large bowls of soup and smaller dishes of fruit salad.

Seated around the table, they reached out to clasp hands

and bowed their heads while Michael asked the Lord's blessing. The telephone rang as they were nearly finished eating. Kate reached out to answer it.

"Mom, I've moved out of the dorm," Danny blurted.

"Why, Danny, what's the matter?" Kate exclaimed in surprise. She straightened stiffly in her chair, then listened in consternation to Danny's quiet weeping.

Her stomach contracted, but she managed to control her panic enough to ask gently, "Danny, what happened?"

Michael and Brenden watched her anxiously. Unable to hear both sides of the conversation, they occasionally looked away to take a token bite, then refocused their eyes intently on Kate's face.

After a minute, Danny pulled himself together. "I didn't want to tell you, Mom, but some of the guys in the dorm have been harassing me."

"What did they do?" Kate asked, gripped by an icy fear. Her mind stopped short of graphically imagining what dreadful thing might have caused Danny to break down.

"At first, it was just writing things like *Danny McLaughlin is a fag!* on the bathroom walls." Kate shuddered at hearing her son's name linked with such an epithet.

"Then a couple of days ago, while I was in the shower, some guys tied the bathroom door shut, and when I tried to open it, they shouted, 'Stay in there, you dirty queer, and don't contaminate our dorm!' " Kate's heart pounded, and dismay swept over her as she swallowed hard against the bitter taste of bile that suddenly filled her mouth.

"I had to wait almost an hour till somebody came by and untied the door. I was so upset I couldn't sleep that night. But today was the worst. I came into the bathroom, and somebody had written 'Death to all fairies! Kill Danny McLaughlin!' in big letters on the wall." Danny's voice was shaking.

"Oh, Danny!" Kate exclaimed. Righteous indignation brought a flush to her cheeks, and fear made her urge, "Somebody should call the police! Did you tell the dean about that?"

"I told him after I got locked in the bathroom, and he said

he'd do something about it, but after today I just couldn't take it anymore."

"It wasn't your roommate, was it?" asked Kate.

"Rob? No, Rob's been great. I think it's two or three freshman guys."

"But, Danny, where did you move to?"

"Well, there're a couple of girls who live in the village, Stacey and Joanna. They're good friends of mine, and they said I could stay with them, at least till I can work something else out."

"Girls?" asked Kate, realizing even as she said it that girls would be safe with Danny.

"Have no fear, Mom," Danny said with a wry chuckle. "They're both lesbians."

"Oh!" said Kate, startled. Then, without stopping to process that thought, she continued, "Well, I think it's a good thing you moved out. This is just terrible. I can't believe young men in a Christian school could be so cruel. I'm so sorry, Danny. I know this must have really upset and hurt you. It hurts all of us. But, honey, I'm afraid some people are just very prejudiced. It would probably be best to be very selective about whom you share this with."

Danny heaved a great sigh. "Yeah, I guess you're right, Mom. Well, let me give you Stacey and Joanna's phone number, in case you need to call me."

After saying goodbye, Kate shakily related the episode to Michael and Brenden.

"Those guys ought to be kicked out of school!" exclaimed Brenden in uncharacteristic anger. "Poor Danny! I feel like writing the dean and telling him what I think about it!"

Kate was gratified by Brenden's spirited defense of his brother. She looked toward Michael to see what his reaction was. He was silent, but Kate was struck by the pained expression on his face. She realized that this was just what he had predicted and knew he wished with all his heart that his predictions hadn't come true.

Chapter 10

Christmas

Winter arrived suddenly the following week. A freezing wind buffeted Kate and Michael as they left the office one evening and hurried through the early darkness to their car.

"A cold front has the eastern third of the nation in its grip," the radio newscaster said, as if he enjoyed broadcasting the depressing news. Kate blew on her fingers. "Temperatures here in the nation's capital reached the low thirties today, but if you thought it felt colder, you were right. With the wind chill, it felt more like ten above."

Michael was the first one up the next morning. "Well, would you look at this!" he said, peering out the window on his way to the bathroom. "The weatherman got caught napping this time."

Suddenly wide awake, Kate joined him at the window to gaze delightedly at a world of white. The wind whipped clouds of snowflakes around the street light.

"Do you suppose they'll close the office?" she asked hopefully. Before Michael could answer, a snowplow clattered by, and they looked at each other in mock resignation.

"Guess I'd better get dressed," she said, turning reluctantly from the window.

"And I guess I'd better shovel out the driveway," added Michael.

As they crept along the snowy roads on the way to work, Michael glanced over at Kate. "I don't know about you, but with winter starting this early, I think I'm going to get awfully tired of cold weather before spring!"

"You're probably right," said Kate, laughing, "but the first snow is always exciting to me."

"If this keeps up, I'll bet you won't think it's so exciting by Christmastime," retorted Michael. "I've got an idea. What would you think of taking a vacation in Hawaii this winter?"

"Oh, that *would* be nice!" exclaimed Kate, her eyes dreamy. "We haven't had a real vacation since we came home from Singapore. And it would be fun seeing all our old friends again."

When they got home that evening, Michael brought a couple of logs in and built a fire in the fireplace. After supper, he and Kate cuddled up on the couch and stared dreamily at the dancing flames.

"Why don't we spend Christmas at Nonnie's with the rest of the family and then fly on to Hawaii for a week?" Michael suggested, returning to the morning's topic of conversation. "Do you have enough vacation time saved up for that?"

"Let's see," Kate said, doing some mental figuring. "Yeah, I think I can manage that, with the Christmas and New Year holidays. I wonder if Brenden would be able to fly out to California for Christmas too. I'd hate to leave him back here by himself."

"Let's ask him," Michael said enthusiastically. "And you know what? Why don't we take Danny with us to Hawaii. It could be an early graduation present. Show him his roots, where he was born, and all that."

Kate's eyes lighted up. "Oh, honey," she said softly, "what a nice idea. That would really be special!"

Michael left the next Friday for some meetings in Canada. After lunch on Sunday, Kate enjoyed a phone call from Alex and his second wife, Stephanie. She especially enjoyed talking to each of her precious little granddaughters. As she hung up, she thought, *I'd better call Danny. He won't want to make any calls on the phone where he's staying.*

She was grateful when Danny answered. "How's it going, buddy?" she asked.

"OK," he answered unconvincingly. "I'm sorta getting settled here. Most of my stuff is packed up and stored at the dorm."

"How is your student teaching going?"

"Well, I didn't do too well on my latest video critique," Danny confessed with a sigh. "I'm having problems with discipline. It's just hard to concentrate on what I'm doing with so many things on my mind."

"That's understandable," sympathized Kate. "Maybe things will go better now that you've moved out of the dorm."

"Yeah."

"Danny, Daddy and I have been talking about taking a week's vacation in Hawaii after Christmas. How would you like to go with us, for a sort of early graduation present?"

"Hey, that would be great!" Danny exclaimed, with some of the old sparkle in his voice. Kate sensed what he didn't say, that the offer was an affirmation of their love that he desperately needed at that moment.

Christmas Eve was the usual noisy hubbub of happy confusion as Nonnie's old house nearly overflowed with the combined families of Michael and his brother and sister—more than two dozen in all. Alex was there with Stephanie, Amy, and Sara and Samantha, Amy's two little half sisters.

Kate, Michael, and Brenden were the last to arrive. Under her excitement, Kate felt a shadow of anxiety about Michael and Danny's first meeting since she had broken the news to Michael.

Looking in the big picture window as they climbed the porch steps, Kate smiled in amusement when she spotted Danny. He was sporting a most remarkable headgear, a flamboyant creation of red velvet that looked like some kind of floppy, oversized beret. Just then, he looked up and saw them. Leaping out of his chair, he ran to the door and flung it open.

"Merry Christmas, Mummy!" he exclaimed, hugging her, then turned to Michael.

"You look like Santa Claus!" chuckled Michael, breaking the ice.

Kate bit her lip as Danny turned and she saw the tiny gold earring. She glanced quickly at Michael, but he seemed not to have noticed. Then Nonnie bustled in, and they were swamped with hugs and greetings.

After Nonnie's bountiful buffet supper, the mob migrated to the family room, where the Christmas tree stood, practically buried under a mountain of gaily wrapped packages. As the evening progressed, Kate observed that Danny was growing unusually quiet and withdrawn. Although no one had said anything, she realized that the family had all noticed Danny's appearance and were drawing their own conclusions. She sensed that it was Danny's way of making a statement and knew he felt the undercurrent of questions and disapproval.

Later, after those who lived near enough had gone home, and sleeping logistics had been figured out for the rest, Kate and Michael got ready for bed. Kate knew Michael had noticed Danny's earring and was irritated, but she hoped he wouldn't say anything. She was disappointed too, but somehow it seemed easier to deal with if nothing was said. This time, she was the one avoiding reality.

Michael got into bed and reached over to turn off the lamp. As he lay back against his pillow, he heaved a big sigh of exasperation.

"Why does Danny have to flaunt this thing and make such a big point of it?" he exclaimed. "Why can't he just keep quiet about it?"

He rolled over on his side and punched angrily at his pillow. "Walt asked me tonight if Danny's gay! Wanted to know if I thought he had AIDS! I didn't know what to say."

Something defensive stirred inside Kate. "Was Walt afraid he might catch AIDS from Danny?" she asked, with a touch of fire in her voice.

Silence reigned for a spell. At last, Kate said in a small, flat voice, "Maybe Danny just needed to know how his family would react when they found out."

Michael didn't answer for several minutes. "Well, he shouldn't expect everybody to act as if nothing has happened," he finally said in a frustrated voice.

Kate looked at the shadows the street light made on the bedroom wall. "I know," she said sadly. "But he's lived with this so long, I suppose it's hard for him to remember that we're just finding out. I think he just needs to know that we all still love him, that our love isn't based on his not being gay."

The next day, Michael insisted that Danny remove his earring. With a stubborn set to his jaw, he silently obeyed. Kate had a sick feeling that their vacation was ruined, but by the time they left for the airport an unspoken truce prevailed, as if they had all decided to enjoy their trip and to avoid talking about "the subject."

As they waited for their flight, Kate could not avoid a stab of pain when she looked at Danny's red nylon carry-on bag with his name stitched on the side. Michael had brought it home from a trip to Korea the year before. Angela had an identical one that she would never use, because it had "Angela McLaughlin" stitched on it. Michael had given them the bags for Christmas, along with the promise of a honeymoon in Hawaii for a wedding present.

A warm, tropical evening greeted them on their arrival in Honolulu. The nearly full moon was rising, illuminating a sky dappled with heaps of cumulus clouds. Palm trees rustled in a gentle breeze that wafted the scent of plumeria blossoms. Pleasant memories mingled with anticipation as they drove across the island to Auntie Florence's home, where they had reserved two rooms. Auntie Florence and Uncle James had been youth leaders in their church for many years. Now, Uncle James was gone, and Auntie Florence had turned her house into a "bed-and-breakfast" facility.

Lazy, sun-filled days passed quickly. Most days were spent on the white, sandy beach at Kailua, where they could look out over the sparkling turquoise waters of the lagoon, the cobalt blue of the deeper ocean beyond the reef, and range after range of purple headlands fading into the distance.

One afternoon they went to the Polynesian Cultural Center to enjoy the music, dances, and culture of the various South Pacific islands. Another day they drove by the house where they had lived many years before and visited the hospital where Danny had been born. Memories of those happy days, when life seemed less complicated, drew the three of them closer together, and they took pleasure in each other's company.

All too soon, they were on the plane headed back to the mainland, leis and fresh tans the only reminder of their tropical holiday. At the airport in San Francisco, they said goodbye as Danny returned to the college, where he had been asked to do another three weeks of student teaching before qualifying for his credentials.

On the flight back to the East Coast, Kate tried not to worry about Danny. He had always been such a good student, but now, at the end of his college career, he seemed to be floundering.

As Kate and Michael talked to him over the next few weeks, it was evident that he wasn't doing too well. Although he tried not to show it, they could tell he was discouraged. So it wasn't too much of a surprise when he called near the end of January and announced that he had decided he didn't want to teach.

"I'll still have my English major, but I don't know what I'll do with it. I just want to get away from here," he told them. "I think I'll see if I can move in with Alex and Stephanie for a while till I can find a job. If I haven't found anything I like by graduation, maybe I'll go to Europe and bum around for a while or something. Maybe I'll even go back out to Singapore. I think I'd like to get in touch with my life out there again. The one thing I do know is that I can't get away from here soon enough."

As she listened to Danny, Kate had the sensation of all her nerves drawing in tightly together, as if shrinking from the pain of this latest disappointment. She could almost see herself holding up both hands to fend off the pain, trying to keep it outside, where it couldn't hurt her.

What's going to happen to Danny? As day followed day, the thought was never absent from Kate's mind. Worry hung over her like a paralyzing pall of uncertainty.

Chapter 11

Steve

Danny had "camped out" with Stacey and Joanna for over two months while finishing his student teaching. Much as he appreciated their taking him in, he knew it was an inconvenience. It was a frustrating, unsettled time, and he was anxious to get out of their way. So it was a relief when he talked to Alex and Stephanie and they graciously offered to let him stay with them while he was job hunting.

He arrived at their small condo on a chilly, rainy afternoon, carrying his bulging suitcase. Stephanie met him at the door, with Samantha on her hip. Sara clung to her mother's leg and made faces at Danny. Beyond them, he could see toys scattered on every surface.

"Come on in," Stephanie greeted, pushing aside a stack of laundry she had been folding so he could sit on the couch. Awkwardly, Danny put his suitcase down by the door and joined her in front of the TV.

"Hi, Uncle Danny," Amy said, glancing up from the cartoons she was watching. Sara climbed onto his lap with her Etch-A-Sketch and demanded that he draw her a picture.

"Hope you don't mind sleeping on the couch," Stephanie said, giving Danny an apologetic smile. "My niece Suzie is staying with us for a while, and she's in the third bedroom. You can hang your clothes in the hall closet."

"Thanks," Danny said. He set Sara on the floor, then got up and opened the closet door. It was nearly full of jackets. He found a few hangers and, opening his suitcase, he took out a couple of shirts and a pair of pants, hung them up, and squeezed them into one end of the closet. Then he closed the suitcase and looked around for some place to put it. Finally, he scooted it up against the end of the couch.

Stephanie got up to fix Samantha a bottle, leaving Danny to watch cartoons and entertain Sara. With a sigh, he leaned back against the couch, noticing a half-eaten peanut-butter-and-jelly sandwich on the armrest just in time.

It was nearly eight-thirty when Alex arrived home, muddy and bone tired after a long day of digging trenches and installing sprinkler systems. Stephanie gave him a loving hug and kiss before handing him the baby and going into the kitchen to start dinner. Cartoons temporarily forgotten, Amy and Sara clamored for their daddy's attention. At last, he dropped down on the couch beside Danny.

"Hey, man! It's good to see you!" he said with an affection-ate grin. "Here's my baby brother, all grown up and finished with college!" Alex gave Danny a friendly slap on his knee, and Danny grinned back, warmed with a comforting sense of "family."

In a little while, Stephanie announced that dinner was ready. She had fixed fried chicken, coleslaw, and baked beans. Alex and Danny had grown up on a vegetarian diet, and although Alex had grown accustomed to eating meat since he and Stephanie were married, Danny had never before tasted any. But he was hungry, and after taking good-sized helpings of beans and coleslaw, he gingerly added a piece of chicken to his plate. When he'd eaten everything else, he cautiously took a small bite of the fried chicken. He was surprised at how chewy and stringy it was. He chewed for a long time, but it never seemed to get chewed up enough to swallow. At last, he surreptitiously put the mouthful back on his plate and decided he wasn't that hungry, after all.

But Alex had noticed. "It's hard to get used to," he commented, "but after a while it tastes pretty good."

Suzie, fifteen, with long, tightly frizzed blond hair, came in about ten o'clock with her boyfriend. Suddenly, the living room seemed noisy and too small, with everyone talking at once over the sound of the TV. Danny gazed around the room at everyone, feeling strangely out of place.

It was late when Suzie's boyfriend finally left. Stephanie was busy getting three sleepy girls ready for bed.

Alex brought Danny a quilt. "I'm afraid we don't have an extra pillow," he apologized.

"That's OK," Danny answered. "I've got my pillow in the car. I'll go get it."

At last, the house quieted down. Danny found a comfortable position on the too-short couch, but it seemed only a moment later when a light from the kitchen awakened him. Opening one eye a crack, he could see Alex standing in front of the open refrigerator. He squinted at his watch. Five minutes past six. He closed his eyes again and tried to go back to sleep. After a bit, the light went off. He heard Alex tell Stephanie goodbye, then the front door closed.

When Danny woke up again, a gray light filled the room. He got up quickly, then saw that the bathroom door was closed and lay back down again.

"Come on, Amy, wake up! The school bus will be here in twenty minutes," urged Stephanie, coming out of the bathroom dragging a sleepy, uncooperative little girl. Danny started to get up again, but the bathroom door closed behind Sara. She came out a minute later, but then Suzie dashed in. Stephanie was still in the bedroom, struggling to get a grumbling Amy dressed. When the bathroom was free at last, Danny hurried in before he lost his chance.

He had forgotten to bring his clothes in with him, so he had to go get them. When he came out twenty minutes later, showered and dressed, he felt almost ready to face the day. The apartment was quiet. Apparently Stephanie had gone back to bed after getting Amy off to school. In the tiny kitchen, Danny found a box of cornflakes. He poured himself a big bowlful, added milk, and sliced a banana.

The first thing to do, he decided after eating, *is to buy a newspaper.* He folded his quilt and laid it over the end of the couch before slipping quietly out the door. Just as it clicked shut, he realized that he didn't have a key.

Oh, well, I can sit in my car to look at the paper, he thought. He drove to the nearby shopping center. Sitting there in the parking lot, he opened the thick newspaper to the Help Wanted ads. Before long, he concluded that there really wasn't any job an English major qualified him for. His computer skills, as well as much of his student employment experience, made some kind of office job his best bet, he decided.

Chewing on his pencil, he studied the positions listed under "Secretarial" and "Administrative Assistant," circling those that looked promising. He looked at his watch. *Nine-thirty. Stephanie should be up by now.* He drove back to the apartment and knocked on the door.

"Well, I wondered what had happened to you," Stephanie said, opening the door.

"I went out to get a newspaper so I could start looking for a job," Danny explained.

"Wow, you're not wasting any time, are you?" laughed Stephanie. Samantha was wailing in the background. " 'Scuse me. I've gotta fix a bottle for the baby."

Danny followed her into the kitchen. "Mind if I use your phone to call about some of these ads?"

"Help yourself," Stephanie said good-naturedly.

The only telephone hung on a wall in the kitchen. Turning his back on the sinkful of dirty dishes, Danny creased the newspaper open and found the first ad he had circled. Taking a deep breath, he lifted the receiver and dialed the number.

"Good morning. Western Graphics," a cool, clipped voice said.

"I'm calling about your ad for an administrative assistant," Danny said in as confident and assured a manner as he could muster.

"I'm sorry, but that position has just been filled." A click signaled the end of the call.

She didn't sound a bit sorry, Danny thought. *Not a very promising beginning.* His eyes moved down to the next ad.

"Redwood Custom Framing." This voice was definitely more friendly.

"I would like to apply for the secretarial position you have advertised in today's paper," Danny said.

"Can you tell me what experience you have had?" asked the friendly voice.

Danny described his previous jobs.

"That sounds good, but have you held any regular, full-time positions since you were a student?" she asked.

Danny had to admit that he hadn't.

"I'm really sorry, but we are looking for someone who's had at least two years' experience in this type of position, so I'm afraid we can't consider you at this time. But good luck in your job hunting!"

Too bad. That sounded like it would have been a nice place to work, Danny thought regretfully as he hung up.

The next firm wanted someone with some accounting experience. After five calls with no results, Danny was beginning to feel pretty discouraged. But the next two calls netted a request to send in his résumé and an actual appointment for an interview.

Feeling elated, he hung up. During the last call, he had been dimly aware of some sort of distraction, and now he realized it was Sara tugging on his pants to get his attention. Swinging her up exuberantly, he went to find Stephanie and share the good news with her.

"Terrific!" she congratulated him. "You'll be a working man before you know it!"

But a wonderful job did not immediately materialize. After several days of following up newspaper ads without success, Danny decided to sign on with an employment agency, as well as a temporary service.

One evening, shortly after moving in with Alex and Stephanie, Danny was browsing through an area of small shops and wandered into a secondhand bookstore, cleverly named Twice-sold Tales. Spotting a table of used classical music tapes, he began looking through them and found one of Smetana's *Má Vlast* that looked interesting.

He took it over to a tall blond man behind the counter. "Could you play a little of this tape for me so I can see what condition it's in?" he requested.

"Certainly!" responded the young man, who, as it turned out, was the store manager. "Do you like Smetana? This is one of my favorites."

Danny smiled. "My mother had a record of this that I remember her playing from the time I was just a little kid. I especially like *The Moldau*. My mom told me the story about the two little streams that joined together to make a big river. I used to sit and look at the picture of the river on the record jacket while I listened to the music."

Danny had been very lonely since he and Mike had decided not to pursue a relationship. He sensed a kindred spirit in Steve, the bookstore manager, and they enjoyed an animated conversation that lasted until time to close the store.

Danny dropped into the bookstore frequently after that, and Steve was always glad to see him. One day Danny stopped by to browse through the children's literature section, looking for ideas for a book he wanted to write. The quiet store held no other customers. Not finding anything he wanted, he stopped to talk to Steve.

"Do you work Sundays?" Danny asked, longing for something to look forward to during this frustrating period of his life.

"No, I have Sundays off," Steve answered. "I sing in the choir at St. Andrew's Church every Sunday morning. Would you like to come and hear the choir sing this Sunday? I think you would enjoy it. Our choir is small but very good, and we sing some great music."

Danny was intrigued. "I'd like that," he agreed enthusiastically. Steve gave him directions.

The following Sunday morning, as the rest of the household slept in, Danny stood in front of the bathroom mirror carefully knotting his maroon knit tie. Pulling on the jacket of his gray pin-stripe suit, he closed the door and ran down the steps to his car.

The church was in a part of town he wasn't familiar with, but Steve's directions were clear. He heard bells pealing as he drove up the street and saw the imposing Spanish Colonial–style building.

A number of people stood on the steps of the church, and Danny saw more coming from all directions. He pulled into a parking spot across the street and got out. Feeling both strangeness and anticipation, he walked up the steps and entered the vaulted nave of the church. A few worshipers were already seated or kneeling in prayer.

Self-conscious, Danny slipped quietly into a pew near the back and looked around, fascinated by the magnificence of the decorations. The dark polished wood of the pews, the slate floor, and the deep red carpet contrasted with the gorgeous stained-glass windows along the side walls and the clerestory. White pillars with beautifully carved moldings supported the clerestory, and gold-tiled walls behind the two side altars reflected the light of flickering candles.

Danny was entranced by the pure, chaste flow of music from the organ loft above and the hushed, reverent atmosphere. Soon people began streaming into the church, as the service was about to begin. Then the sweet, ethereal voices of the choir singing the introit came floating down from the balcony, and Danny caught his breath at its beauty. The minister, in flowing black clerical robes richly trimmed with velvet, approached the main altar, and the congregation knelt as he began to pray. The service consisted largely of Scripture and liturgy, read responsively by the minister and the people.

When the service was over, Steve, wearing a black cassock and white surplice, found Danny and invited him to come and meet the rest of the choir. Danny was surprised to discover how small it was. The live acoustics of the church made twelve voices sound like a much larger group.

"The music was just beautiful!" Danny exclaimed. "I'd love to sing in a choir like this!"

"Well, come join us!" Steve invited enthusiastically. "Are you a tenor or baritone?"

"Baritone," Danny answered.

"That's just what we need!" Turning to the organist/choir director, Steve announced, "Marilyn, Danny's a baritone, and he'd like to join the choir." Turning back to Danny, he amended, "Wouldn't you?"

"Why . . . , of c-course, if I could," Danny stammered eagerly.

Marilyn and the other choir members were very friendly and encouraging, and Danny agreed to come to rehearsal on Wednesday evening.

Later, standing on the steps of the church, Steve asked, "Would you like to eat lunch with me? I know a great little French restaurant down on the square."

Delighted, Danny followed Steve in his car. La Gare was small and rustic looking, with wooden floors, lace curtains, tin lanterns on round tables covered with blue-checked cloths, and pots of geraniums in the windows.

They were seated near a window. Steve studied the menu for a moment. "The *poulet roti* is very good," he suggested. "Or if you prefer something lighter, they make delicious omelets."

"That sounds good," Danny said quickly. He wasn't really that fond of omelets, but he preferred them to chicken.

"Try the *omelette aux champignon*," Steve advised. "You'll love it."

Three years older than Danny, Steve seemed very sure of himself. As they ate, he told Danny about his hobby of gourmet cooking and his musical studies with a well-known Bay-area musician. He played both the piano and organ, and besides singing at St. Andrew's, he sometimes substituted for the cantor at the Russian Orthodox Church. Danny was impressed and a little intimidated by how knowledgeable Steve was about classical music.

"Have you ever done any two-piano music?" Danny asked. "I'd love to play 'Scaramouche' with you sometime." To his surprise, Steve wasn't familiar with the piece.

"It's by Milhaud, and it's full of these stirring Latin rhythms and dreamy impressionism," Danny said enthusiastically. "I learned it when I was in high school, and it's so much fun to play. One of my classmates and I played the last movement for a talent program and won first prize."

"I'd like to try it," Steve said. "But where could we find two pianos?"

"Maybe we could find a studio with two pianos in the music building up at my college," Danny suggested. "Anyway, my stuff's still all stored up there, so we'd have to go there to get my music."

They decided to drive to the college that afternoon. After rummaging through an untidy box filled with books and music, Danny finally found what he was looking for, and they headed for the music building. After Steve had read through his part a few times, they tried it together.

"Hey, this is really great!" Steve exclaimed. "No wonder you like it!" Danny glowed, both from the fun of playing one of his favorite pieces and from Steve's approval.

As the weeks turned into months, Danny's job search continued to be disappointing. He made it to the final interview for several promising jobs, but the other finalist was always selected because of having more experience. And most of his temporary jobs were boring "dead ends."

As kind as Alex and Stephanie were, he was getting very tired of living out of a suitcase, sleeping on the couch, and sharing a bathroom with six other people. He longed to get settled in a place of his own. He began studying the ads for rentals and checked some of them out, even though he knew it was an impossible dream until he had a steady job.

At last, after three months, he took a temporary job with the office of the city water district that looked as if it might develop into something permanent.

Meanwhile, Danny's friendship with Steve was growing into something deeper. One evening, Steve suggested that maybe Danny would like to move in with him. He was living in a house owned by a man who traveled overseas much of the year. Because he kept the house up while the owner was away, his rent was only $150 a month.

"If you move in with me, we can split the rent," Steve said. "Don probably wouldn't like it if he knew you were living with me, but he won't be back for almost a year."

Accepting Steve's offer, Danny realized his feelings included more than just relief over getting into a place of his own.

Chapter 12

AIDS Conference

The April afternoon was surprisingly mild, and Kate rolled down her window to enjoy the gentle breezes as she drove into the city. The arching loveliness of blossoming pear trees along the grassy strip dividing the street reminded her of spring break just a year ago and the fresh pain of her discovery about Danny's homosexuality.

It seemed as though she had lived a whole lifetime since then, she thought with a sigh. What an undreamed-of world of pain she had uncovered in that year!

And now she was on her way to open a new chapter in her education. She remembered her surprise the week before when she had read the announcement in her church bulletin. One of the large churches in the city was sponsoring an AIDS conference. The fact that the church was going to discuss something like this openly seemed almost incredible!

At the stoplight, Kate closed her eyes for a moment, reveling in the warmth of sunlight on her face. *Of course*, she reflected, *it is probably easier for the church to tackle the problem of AIDS than to acknowledge that a sizable minority of its members have to deal with a homosexual orientation.*

As the light changed and traffic moved on, Kate thought about those few she had found the courage to confide in over the past year—Dr. Zimmerman, her pastors, Greg and Laura, and two or three other close friends. In every case, she had been happily surprised by their understanding and support.

But she had also sensed their discomfort. She had such an urgent need to talk to someone, to discuss her questions and her fears. How often she had yearned for someone just to ask, "How's it going, Kate?" and give her an opportunity to express her feelings. But none of them had ever attempted to bring up the subject again, and she was reluctant to mention it herself.

The church is uncomfortable too, she thought as she turned the corner and saw the stately granite façade of the church, softened by clouds of pink cherry blossoms.

Over the year, she had begun to realize how many families harbored this painful secret, and it troubled her that the church seemed to be doing nothing to acknowledge their pain or to offer any real help for those struggling with a sexual-identity crisis.

Driving into the parking lot, Kate was amazed to see how full it was. She was nearly five minutes late, but she had planned it that way. As she dropped her keys into her black patent-leather shoulder bag and opened the door, a feeling of vulnerability swept over her. It almost seemed as though she was making a public announcement by attending this meeting. But she also felt a strange sense of anticipation at the opportunity to see others who had some reason to be interested in the topic of the conference.

Straightening the pleated skirt of her yellow suit, she crossed the street and climbed the broad steps of the church, grateful that no one else was in sight. She picked up a program from the table in the narthex and opened the door to the sanctuary. There were a number of empty seats on the far right side.

Gathering her courage, she walked down the aisle and slipped into a pew as inconspicuously as possible. A quick glance around assured her that no one she knew was sitting nearby.

Seated behind a table on the platform she saw three men, who were being introduced by Karen Marshall, one of the editors of the church's general journal.

The first, Mario Rivas, was tall, lanky, and boyish looking, his sandy hair curling engagingly over his forehead. He had grown up attending church school and had been a nurse for fourteen years.

Next to him sat a dark-haired young man with striking good looks. John Lawson, thirty-two years old, was a legal analyst for a large national corporation and had grown up in a minister's home.

The third member of the panel was an older man, Richard Hansen, who had enjoyed a successful career as an administrator of hospitals, including two of the largest hospitals in Los Angeles. He was pale and appeared to be ill. Mario and John were HIV-positive; Richard had been diagnosed two years earlier with AIDS.

In a soft, gentle voice with a Spanish accent, Mario began telling his story. "I had adopted a pseudonym to use this weekend," he admitted, "but when I got here and began using it, it didn't feel natural, so I have taken my name back." The audience chuckled.

Mario said that after finishing school, he had become engaged, because that was what was expected in his culture. But as the wedding drew near, he felt very uncomfortable and confused. He was afraid to get married but didn't know what to do, so he prayed that if the marriage wasn't meant to be, God would stop it. Shortly after that, his fiancée broke up with him, and immediately, his fear and confusion left him. The very same day, he met the man who became his lover.

"I am very fortunate," Mario said softly, "that I have shared a loving relationship with my mate for fourteen years."

Kate's heart was pounding as she listened to Mario. His story was so much like Danny's. Hearing him tell about his experience brought Danny's feelings more vividly to life for her. Mario's description of his relationship with his lover awakened conflicting feelings of sympathy and revulsion in Kate. She couldn't help thinking of Danny and Steve.

Mario told how frightening it had been to learn that he was HIV-positive. It had been a growing experience, he said, as he learned to accept life on its own terms. His spiritual experience, especially, had deepened. He had gone to friends and family members who had rejected him and had forgiven them so he would be able to die in peace.

John was the next to speak. While Mario had the soft, gentle way about him that Kate had come to associate with homosexual men, John was very masculine looking and had a rich, deep voice. He was using a pseudonym, he said, because he had not yet told his parents that he was gay and HIV-positive, although he planned to do so very soon.

"Fourteen years ago," he recalled, "as a high-school senior visiting the nation's capital, I attended this church and sat up there in the balcony looking down at this platform, never dreaming that one day I would be sitting here addressing you on such a topic."

His story, too, gave Kate new insights into Danny's experience. "As the son of a minister, I grew up in an extremely conservative environment," he told them. "I recognized at an early age that I had sexual tendencies very different from my peers. At that age—four or five—you believe you're the only one like that, and it makes you very secretive. Later, as a teenager, I went through many guilt feelings as I tried to correlate my sexual desires with my religious training.

"When I went away to college, I somehow came in contact with Kinship, and that was the turning point of my life. I have never experienced such unconditional love anywhere as I did with Kinship.

"I finally understood that my orientation was not a choice, and I learned to accept myself for what I was. It's absurd to think anyone would *choose* to be different, would *choose* to be excluded and persecuted, would *choose* to have his family ashamed of him!

"Tell me," John demanded, looking out at the audience, "exactly when did you *choose* to be a heterosexual?"

Kate shivered and felt goosebumps break out on her arms as she, with the rest of the audience, listened to his challenge in shocked silence.

Richard's story was the saddest of all. He had been married and the father of two sons, when marital problems and his disturbing sexual thoughts led him to seek counsel from his pastor. Far from helping him, the pastor later broke confidence and testified against him when his wife divorced him and sought custody of their boys.

In a passive voice that displayed pain rather than anger, he told of being summarily terminated from his $150,000-a-year job as a hospital administrator when he was diagnosed with AIDS. His sons had asked seven different pastors to visit him when he was hospitalized, but none would come. The IRS immediately froze all his assets, and he lost his two houses and two cars.

"I would have been living on the street if Kinship had not given me $500 a month for over a year," he told them, in a voice that trembled with emotion.

Kate's attention had been totally focused on the speakers, but as Karen Marshall stepped to the microphone to thank them for their courage in sharing their personal experiences, she relaxed a little and looked around at the others in the audience. She saw a number of people she knew scattered throughout the church. She was struck by the intensity of interest evident in people's faces and demeanor.

Kate turned her attention back to the program. "AIDS: Our Response" was the topic of the next panel. Dr. Ben Moore, an associate pastor of the church, introduced the panel members.

It was a very distinguished group, including a university president and a physician who was chief of infectious services at a large California hospital.

Dr. Moore asked each of them to take approximately five minutes to sum up what they had shared during the previous two days of the conference and where they felt the church needed to go from there.

The air seemed charged with electric tension as the panelists spoke. One after another, they called on the church to take the lead in showing God's love to AIDS sufferers.

Unconsciously, Kate leaned forward, her eyes riveted on the panelists. Even though the word *homosexual* was not used, Kate felt it was implied.

A social-services professional from Chicago told them,

"Those who have left our church still long to be a part of us. We are their family, and they have a strong bond with us. Do they feel caring and compassion from us, their church family?"

The editor of a church magazine for blacks, a tall, nice-looking, articulate young man, mentioned that hearing the stories of painful discrimination from those with AIDS had touched him deeply because he was sensitive to discrimination.

"The church," he said, "must be challenged to put itself in someone else's situation. We have to think, *How would I feel? What would I want someone to do for me?*"

"Is the church afraid to get involved with AIDS for fear that its resources will be diverted from evangelism?" the state health officer of Delaware asked. "We need to realize that the only way many people will see our God is by the way we show His love."

Spontaneous applause greeted his words, and Kate joined in, hesitantly at first, then more strongly.

One speaker did bring the implied out in the open. The doctor from California spoke about how families often get the news that a son (1) is gay and (2) has AIDS at nearly the same time.

"The church should have a ministry of providing a supportive atmosphere for this kind of painful revelation," he challenged.

He closed with an impassioned appeal for the church to fight discrimination in any form, as both immoral and illegal. Kate felt her blood stir as she applauded vigorously.

In her concentration, Kate had rolled her program into a tight scroll. As Dr. Moore again came to the microphone, she leaned back in her seat and took a deep breath. Unrolling her program, she saw that a question-and-answer period was next.

A young man wearing black slacks and a white shirt with rolled-up sleeves stood alertly at the front of the church, ready to carry a microphone to those who wanted to ask questions. Soon a number of people were standing, waiting their turn to speak.

One older woman, standing near the back of the church, spoke with a foreign accent. Dr. Moore asked her to repeat her question.

"One of the young men said people with AIDS need to be hugged."

"I'm sorry. They need what? Did you say *help?*" asked Dr. Moore in a puzzled voice.

"No, a *hug. H-u-g!*" exclaimed the woman. "I would like to hug somebody with AIDS." Although Dr. Moore was still having difficulty understanding her, Mario caught what she was saying and, jumping up, he ran down the aisle with his arms outstretched. Comprehension dawned on Dr. Moore's face, and he began laughing delightedly, joined by the rest of the audience, as Mario and the woman embraced.

A young woman stood on the other side of the large church, but it wasn't until she began talking that Kate realized it was a woman she knew from her church. She spoke slowly, in a husky, emotion-filled voice.

"You mentioned that we can get involved by becoming a 'buddy' to someone with AIDS. I have been a buddy to a man with AIDS for almost a year. Last Tuesday, my buddy died . . . , and his funeral was this afternoon."

She stopped a moment, then went on. "I wasn't able to go to his funeral, but I am glad I can be here at this conference. My question is this: Does our church have any kind of a support system so I can find a member of my church who has AIDS to be a buddy to?"

An electric silence followed her question. Kate chewed her lip as she waited tensely for a response.

When no one on the panel spoke, Dr. Moore said, "I guess I will have to speak to that question. Unfortunately, the answer is No. We *do* have an AIDS Concerns group in this church, but we have been prevented from ministering effectively, because people in our church find it difficult to admit that they need help. There is still far too much suspicion and judgmentalism in the church. It is tragic that in a world where we all struggle with sin, and sinfulness, people should still feel rejected by the church!"

Kate clenched and unclenched her fists, feeling like a spring that was wound too tightly. She almost jumped when the doctor's low, quiet voice broke the silence.

"We passed over the lady's question too quickly, Ben. I'm sorry. It was a simple question. Out of—how many church members do we have in North America? Out of 750,000 members, is there . . . *any* . . . support group?" He spoke slowly, emphatically. "I think we need some silence as we contemplate—*No! Not . . . one!*"

Kate's lips quivered, and tears spilled unheeded down her cheeks.

"Is that not . . . *painful?*" continued the doctor's passionate, probing voice. "Do we not feel some . . . *horror?*"

It was to a subdued and thoughtful audience that Dr. Moore made a concluding announcement.

"You have heard several references made this afternoon to 'The Quilt,' " he said. "I'm not sure how many of you are familiar with what is known as the AIDS Quilt Project. Some of us went down to the quadrangle in front of the White House where 'The Quilt' was spread out recently.

" 'The Quilt' is a series of panels, about three feet by six feet in size, all stitched together. Each panel represents at least one person who has died from AIDS. 'The Quilt' is now so large—it is *acres*—that this is the last time it can be spread out on the quadrangle.

"Kinship has put together its own quilt. It is a striking quilt, because it contains the names of a number of church members who have died of AIDS. If you would like to see this quilt, it will be on display after the meeting, in the pastors' lounge."

Kate was seized with a compelling desire to see the Kinship Quilt. Even though she didn't think Danny was promiscuous, she had never been able to rid herself of the fear that he might get AIDS.

Will he someday be represented by a three-by-six-foot panel? she wondered.

As people stood and began to leave the church, Kate remained in her seat, struggling with a decision. She had managed to remain anonymous so far, but if she went to see the quilt, she ran a greater risk of being seen by someone she knew. But she could feel the quilt drawing her, and she could not leave without seeing it.

When Kate entered the pastors' lounge, twenty or thirty people stood silently contemplating the large quilt, which was draped over two couches in the center of the room. From the moment she caught sight of the quilt, Kate stood transfixed, unable to tear her eyes away.

Rather than a series of panels, it was a single large quilt. In one corner was appliqued a miniature green scrub suit and a stethoscope beside the name of a doctor, the most recent Kinship member to die of AIDS. A bunch of colorful balloons was embroidered above another name, obviously someone with a lighthearted love of life.

Kate stared at the quilt for a long time.

On a bright, breezy afternoon five months later, Kate walked the corridors of San Francisco's International Airport, waiting to transfer to the next leg of her flight on a long-anticipated visit to Singapore.

Her attention was drawn to colorful banners hanging from the ceiling. She wondered idly if they had been created by schoolchildren. They reminded her vaguely of the mats her boys had taken to kindergarten for their naptime. They were about the same size. . . . Each banner seemed to have a name on it. . . .

With an awful fascination, Kate walked closer. She could feel her skin beginning to prickle. A bright blue panel hung in front of her. In the center, a brown-and-white beagle was appliqued. A row of red and yellow tulips marched across the bottom. Big green letters at the top of the banner proclaimed "ALLEN—June 13, 1952, to May 7, 1987."

Beyond it was a yellow panel decorated with a piano keyboard and a music staff with notes. It bore the name "STEVEN" and the dates "July 3, 1958–July 2, 1990."

She turned to stare blindly out the window as a great sob rose from somewhere deep inside.

Chapter 13

Graduation

On a day nearly two months after the AIDS Conference, Kate tore a page off the calendar and stared at the picture of a mountain lake, framed by tall firs. *June.* Danny's graduation was only three weeks away. For a moment, panic gripped her.

Against her will, she had begun to accept the fact that a relationship was developing between Danny and Steve.

With his father, however, Danny was much more reticent about mentioning Steve, and Michael seemed unaware of any such development. He was still convinced that Danny was just going through a phase, and Kate had not had the heart to try to share her unwelcome knowledge with him.

But what will happen when he sees the evidence with his own eyes? she wondered uneasily. Her apprehension grew as she imagined Michael's reaction when he realized that Danny and Steve were more than just roommates.

Kate turned away from the calendar and looked with a frown at the page she had unconsciously crumpled in her hand. She smoothed out the picture of rose and purple azaleas that she had meant to save for her bulletin board, then shrugged and tossed it in the trash.

In an automatic gesture, she rubbed her hand back and forth across her abdomen; her stomach felt tied up in knots all the time. She reached up to massage the tenseness from the back of her neck.

I'm so tired, she thought. *Seems like I haven't had a good night's sleep for weeks.* Her depression that, for a while, had lifted a little once again clouded her life with hopelessness.

Just three more weeks until one of the most important milestones in Danny's life—his graduation from college. This should be an exciting time of celebration, but instead, Kate looked forward to it with dread. Underneath was a dull anger that all the joy had been sucked out of this event.

And, of course, there'll be no wedding to look forward to, she reminded herself glumly. *No grandchildren.*

She knew Danny was eager for her to meet Steve. "You'll really like him, Mom!" he had assured her in his last phone call. "The two of you have so much in common."

Kate could detect a wistful undertone to his enthusiasm. *I'm not at all sure, Danny,* she thought. *I'm not sure what my reaction will be to Steve. But what I am sure of is that you need our love and support more than ever now. I'll just have to make the best of the situation.*

Nevertheless, as she and Michael settled into their aisle seats across from each other on a mid-June morning, Kate comforted herself that in less than a week they would be back home again, and the long-dreaded moment, for better or for worse, would be behind them.

As the plane took off, she opened her purse and pulled out a plastic bag containing brilliant triangles of scarlet, royal blue, purple, and black. Putting her mind in neutral, she began piecing them together to make blocks for Danny's quilt.

Stephanie and the girls met them at the airport in San Francisco. As soon as they got to Alex and Stephanie's condo, Kate called Danny. He had just gotten home from work.

"Tell you what," he suggested. "Why don't Steve and I meet the rest of you at The Good Earth for supper?"

"That sounds like a good idea," agreed Kate, with a sense of fatalistic inevitability. "Shall we meet you there in about an hour?"

Playing with three little granddaughters and visiting with Alex and Stephanie helped Kate keep her mind off the impending encounter. Alex, who instinctively recognized her apprehension, patted her arm and whispered, "Don't worry,

Mom. Steve's a nice guy. You'll like him."

Somehow, that reassured her a little. And she realized she was growing eager to see Danny again, no matter what.

The restaurant had large half-moon windows fronting the street. Chattering and laughing, their entourage made its way inside. Kate took a deep breath, looked around, and spotted Danny sitting on a bench beside a tall, rather large man with curly blond hair, twinkling green eyes, and an engaging smile.

They stood up, and Danny introduced Steve to his parents. As Kate shook Steve's moist hand, she realized that he was nervous too. Her maternal instincts awakened, she knew that her job was to put Steve and Danny at ease.

"Let's see if we can sit upstairs on the balcony," Danny suggested.

Soon they were seated around a long table overlooking the courtyard below. "What do they have here for vegetarians?" asked Michael, opening his menu.

"Oh, they make a delicious broccoli-cheese soup," offered Steve eagerly. "And there's a very nice vege-sandwich too. Danny likes that, I know."

Kate was surprised at how easy it was to like Steve. He was a good conversationalist, and she enjoyed talking to him. Animatedly, he discussed his favorite composers, punctuating his remarks by pushing his glasses up on his nose. Meanwhile, Michael and Danny were engrossed in reviewing the many problems Danny was having with his car.

Midway through the meal, Kate looked around at the happy family group with a slight sense of unreality. Everything seemed so normal and ordinary. Time passed quickly, and it was late when they walked back to their cars through the warm spring evening.

The next afternoon, Kate and Michael picked Danny up at his office, and they drove up to the college for a special supper honoring the seniors and their parents.

One of Danny's classmates was a Chinese girl he had gone to school with in Singapore. Cheryl's father was a doctor at the hospital there. Cheryl and her parents were the first ones they spotted as they entered the cafeteria. Enthusiastically, Michael went over to greet them, with Kate and Danny following. Michael didn't seem to notice anything, but Kate thought she detected a certain stiffness and restraint as Dr. and Mrs. Ho returned his greeting. When she sensed that the Hos were not anxious to prolong the conversation, she steered Michael toward some other friends they had not seen for years. Glancing back, she saw Cheryl and her parents engaged in deep conversation as they looked her way.

"Do they know?" she asked Danny in a low voice.

"I'm sure they do," he answered. "I roomed with Cheryl's brother last year, remember?

On the way home that evening, they discussed plans for the next day. "I expect you'll want to go to church up at the college tomorrow, won't you?" Michael asked.

"Yeah," Danny agreed. "And I think Steve might come too."

Kate was aware that Danny had attended his own church very seldom during the past year. He had also told her that he was singing in the choir at Steve's church every week. *At least he still feels a bond to our church*, she thought gratefully.

"I've fixed potato salad and sandwiches and stuff so we could have a picnic lunch after church," she offered.

"Hey, that's great, Mom!" Danny exclaimed, smiling. "We can eat down at Alumni Park."

Once again, Kate experienced that strange sense of unreality as she sat between Michael and Danny the following morning in church, with Steve on the other side of Danny. She found herself trying to see the church through Steve's eyes. The soft light, muted to gold by stained glass, and dark walnut pews padded in wine velvet gave a dignified, reverent ambience; the music of organ and choir was rich and glorious; the sermon was challenging and thought provoking. Did it seem that way to Steve too? To Danny?

How many of Danny's friends, to whom he had "come out," were looking curiously at them? Kate wondered.

It was a perfect summer day—warm and sunny, with a bit of breeze—as they drove to Alumni Park after church. Danny and Steve carried the picnic hamper and ice chest to a table while Michael got a couple of lawn chairs out of the trunk. Kate looked around at the little park as she followed the winding path up the hill. Angela and Danny had once considered the possibility of an outdoor wedding here, she remembered painfully. Was Danny remembering that too?

Kate had heard about Steve's gourmet cooking from Danny, and she felt a bit intimidated, so she was gratified to see that he seemed to like her tasty, but simple, meal. Sitting in the shade of a huge live oak tree, they enjoyed the pleasant afternoon long after they had finished eating.

The campus overflowed with throngs of friends and relatives and black-gowned graduates when they arrived early the next morning.

In the parking lot, Kate helped Danny slip into his robe and adjusted his mortarboard to the proper angle before giving him a hug and kissing his bearded cheek.

They headed toward the gymnasium, where the commencement exercises were to begin in half an hour. Danny found his place in line while Michael, Kate, and Steve hurried inside to find seats. Since each graduate was allowed only four reserved seats, Alex and his family had decided to stay home.

The auditorium buzzed with excited conversation as the huge crowd waited for the festivities to begin. At last, the organist began a stately processional, and everyone turned toward the back doors as faculty members, in their colorful academic regalia, began marching down the center aisle.

Michael took his camera out of its bag and left to find a position near the back entrance where he could take Danny's picture as he entered with the rest of the seniors. For a moment, Kate felt awkward, sitting there alone with Steve. But the moment passed, and they were soon chatting easily.

When the service was finally over and the nearly four hundred graduates had all received their diplomas, they formed a line to receive congratulations in the guadrangle around the reflecting pool. Michael happily snapped away a roll of film.

They were back in their cars, heading down to the valley.

As they drove through the first town, Michael pulled up at the side of the road, and Danny stopped behind him. Michael got out and went back to talk to Danny.

"Do you guys know a good restaurant around here?" he asked. "I don't know about you, but I'm getting hungry, and I think we should take you out to celebrate!"

Danny grinned. "I was just thinking the same thing!" he responded. "There's a good Italian place up this next street. I'll lead the way."

Bosco's was a quaint, crowded little place with atmosphere. They had to wait for an empty table on the sawdust-covered floor. Steve recommended the fettucini alfredo, and they had *gelatio* for dessert.

Kate's heart felt giddy with relief. It was over, and it had gone well! Nothing had marred this day that was meant to be happy. Either Michael had not noticed anything unusual about Danny and Steve's relationship, or he had chosen to ignore it. Kate sent a bewildered, but grateful, little prayer of thanks heavenward.

"Danny, you need a more dependable car," Michael proclaimed as they were finishing their dessert. "Let's stop at that lot by the fairgrounds where people park cars they're trying to sell."

Kate felt sure that this had not been part of Danny's plans for the day. She knew how he liked to procrastinate on big decisions like this. But she also knew that if Michael had made up his mind this was what needed to be done, nothing was going to stop him.

Danny had to be fed up with all the car trouble he'd been having. And since he'd never shown much interest in anything mechanical, he probably realized that his dad knew a lot more about cars than he did, so Kate wasn't too surprised when he acquiesced gracefully. Steve, however, wasn't interested in an afternoon of car shopping, so Kate offered to take him home.

If there was one pastime besides golf that Michael really enjoyed, it was shopping for used cars. He spent a happy afternoon checking out every car on the lot as Danny trailed around after him, alternating between interest and boredom.

"This Plymouth Colt is definitely the best deal here," he announced at last, patting the hood of a sporty-looking little fire-engine-red car they had just taken out for a test drive.

"It's in good shape and clean as a whistle. If you have it serviced regularly, it should last you for a long time."

Michael folded his arms across his chest and, leaning back against the car, looked at Danny. "What do you want to do?"

A warm wave of gratitude for his dad's concern and practical kind of love washed over Danny. "I think I'd like to buy it, Dad," he conceded with a grin.

"It's a sharp-looking car," Michael said enthusiastically. "But there's one thing you'd better remember," he warned. "Cops are on the lookout for red cars, so don't break any traffic laws, or you'll get caught for sure!

"I could get a loan application from the bank tomorrow morning, and we could go to the bank during your lunch hour," he suggested as they got back into Danny's old Renault. "There shouldn't be any problem getting it approved. Then we can go over and pick up the car after you get off work."

Danny turned toward Michael before putting the key in the ignition. "Thanks a lot, Dad," he said warmly. "I really appreciate your help."

"Danny . . ." The urgency in Michael's voice halted Danny as he was about to turn the key. He looked back at his dad.

At Bosco's, Kate had thought perhaps Michael hadn't noticed anything unusual about Danny and Steve's relationship. She was wrong.

"Danny," he said earnestly, "you're still young. It's not too late to change. You don't have to live this kind of life. You can get some help."

Danny stared painfully at his dad for a minute, then turned away with a sigh. He shook his head. "You just don't understand, Dad," he said in frustration. He started the engine. "I'm sorry. I wish it were that simple."

They drove back to Alex and Stephanie's in silence.

Chapter 14

Ups and Downs: Letters From Danny

October 15 . . . Steve and I have been doing some house hunting the last couple of weeks, and a good thing too. Don, the man whose house we have been staying in, called last night and told Steve he's had a change in plans and will be coming home next month.

Steve is in a panic because he hasn't told Don about me staying here. He told Don that he is planning to move out before he gets back, so now we have to act fast.

We've found a nice little house for rent that's actually closer to work for both of us. We went over today after work and signed a lease. Now, we have to get busy packing. . . .

November 9 . . . We're finally getting somewhat organized, although the garage is still full of boxes. Nonnie let me have an old couch and chair, because she just bought new furniture for her living room, so we're fixed up quite comfortably. She also let me have the old refrigerator she had out in her garage, and we bought a card table and two folding chairs at a garage sale. Our biggest expense was a new queen-size bed.

Two cats have been hanging around ever since we moved in. The neighbors say the people who lived here before abandoned them, so we have adopted them. We call them, very originally, Black Kitty and White Kitty! White Kitty, especially, is very affectionate. . . .

December 3 . . . Work! What a disgusting revelation the

"real" world is. The office here at the water district is constantly filled with petty squabbles that either build to huge, hate-filled confrontations (as it is now), or settle into a simmering fear in which everyone acts terribly polite and avoids looking at each other, and you know things can't go on like this much longer. Well, I can't say I haven't learned a lot about survival this year! . . .

December 14 . . . We came out to Bill and Mark (the other gay couple in the choir) last night. We thought they probably already knew about us, but apparently they didn't. Bill seemed especially surprised; his jaw almost dropped off his face!

It was really hard for Steve to muster up his courage to tell them. He's only come out to a couple of other people in his life. But it all turned out very well. Bill and Mark were delighted, and we talked and talked and talked until nearly midnight. It was very good . . .

January 1 . . . We've decided to rent a piano. We'll put it in our second bedroom, where we have a desk and all our books, and that will become our music studio/library. . . .

February 11 . . . You asked where I am spiritually. Well, I'm as uncertain and unsettled as ever. I don't know what I want or how to distinguish it from my fears or whether either one has any bearing on truth or whether anything even matters at all.

I certainly wouldn't care to live this past year over again; too many bad things have happened to me. There have been so many things that have made me afraid, and I feel like I've gradually retreated back into some little crevice of my soul until only my eyes are exposed to the cruel world. I think I've become very right-brained this past year. I'm not at all sure I'm pleased about it, but nevertheless that is what has happened.

Things seem to swim in a fog of emotions and impressions. It's hard to really see anything. Very much like a dream. It's not as bad as it was, though. For a while, I was under such terrible pressures from all sides that I was unable to remember things I was supposed to do at work, or I'd leave words out of sentences or forget to turn off my car lights. Things are somewhat better now. . . .

March 27 . . . The weather has been absolutely gorgeous the last few weeks, and I have SPRING FEVER! I have planted nasturtiums, sweet peas, and morning glories in our tiny, tiny backyard, and I am going to have an herb garden, as well, so Steve can have all the fresh herbs he wants for cooking. I hope you'll be coming out to visit this summer. I can't wait to show you my garden. . . .

June 2 . . . It's been nearly a year since Steve and I first made our commitment to each other. Our relationship so far has been through a lot of hard times, but I believe we have worked through them well. I am so glad I have someone I can share my life with. . . .

August 10 . . . Your visit was wonderful! It gave me a warm, gooshy feeling inside and reminded me of all the good memories I have of my childhood.

I'm fascinated by the quilt you're making me, Mom. It's exciting to think that it's your very own original design. I definitely think you ought to enter it in a quilt show when it's finished. I don't mind that you're putting it aside while you make a quilt for Brenden and Melissa's wedding. I'll just enjoy the anticipation of receiving it someday in the future.

It meant a lot to me that you came to hear our choir sing. I knew you would be impressed with its quality. I don't imagine it was particularly comfortable for you to attend St. Andrew's, but I appreciate your being willing, and especially for coming up to the choir loft afterward and meeting everyone. . . .

September 7 . . . I went to see a doctor about the pain in my arms, and he said it's tendinitis. My job is about 90 percent data entry, and my work station has not been ideal. I've made some changes to improve it, and the doctor had me get splints for both of my arms. . . .

September 21 . . . My doctor told me I have to cut back to working part time for a while, as my tendinitis isn't getting any better. Workmen's Comp will recompense me for the time I miss. I certainly can't say I'll be unhappy to spend less time under this racklike tension. . . .

October 11 . . . I'm working just till one o'clock every day. In case you're wondering what I'm doing with all my spare time, I have really gotten into composing. I got interested in that last year, you know, but now I am getting serious. I have started composing a cantata, based on the sixty-first Psalm. I have the first chorus, "Hear My Cry, O God!" half finished already. Next time you call, I'll play it for you over the phone. . . .

November 2 . . . Steve left yesterday for the conference in Scotland. He'll be gone for two weeks. I'll miss him, but it'll be good to be alone for a while. We were beginning to get on each other's nerves.

I guess what bothers me most about Steve is that he doesn't seem to value me as a person. He isn't interested in my opinions, my likes and dislikes, my life before we met. It seems like he has never learned how to give and take. Everything has to be done his way. It is a very lopsided relationship.

I shall have lots of time to work on my cantata. I'm glad you liked the first chorus when I played it for you the other day. I've almost finished a tenor aria, "From the Ends of the Earth I Call to You," and then I will start another chorus, "Lead Me to the Rock." . . .

November 25 . . . When I went to see my doctor last week, he said I'm going to have to quit working entirely for probably a couple of months to see if my tendinitis will clear up. If not,

I could be permanently disabled. If I am permanently disabled, Workmen's Comp will pay for my retraining for a new job. . . .

March 16 . . . Here's the tape of my cantata. It's from the rehearsal; the one we recorded at the performance didn't turn out, unfortunately. Marilyn, our organist and choir director, was quite pleased with it.

My final diagnosis is partial disability. I have to find a job where I will be doing computer entry no more than 60 percent of the time. I'm working on updating my résumé and will be trying to find something as an administrative assistant. Workmen's Comp will continue paying me for up to six months, if it takes that long to find a job.

June 5 . . . Tahoe was a little bit of heaven! It was really great of you to rent that house on the lake and invite all of us to come. It was wonderful to relax, play games, go for walks, and best of all, just to be together as a family again and talk and remember old times. I'll never forget it!

I wish I could have stayed for the whole week, but Steve was being difficult. Since he was borrowing my car while his was in the shop, I thought he could have gone out of his way a little to pick me up on Sunday, but he would have had to make arrangements for another cantor to take his place. Anyway, what's done is done, but I'm glad for the time I had with you. . . .

July 24 . . . My interview went well. It sounds like a very interesting job. It's a group of environmental scientists. I would be working directly under one of them—a woman, by the way—but would also be available for two other scientists when they need extra help. There is a fair amount of creativity involved with producing reports, and I would learn several new computer programs. Fortunately, there isn't a lot of data entry. . . .

I got the job! Dr. Johnson called and said I was far more qualified than any of the other candidates, and she was impressed with my computer skills. Said I was better than anybody they'd had working there in the ten years she'd been with the company. I start next Monday. . . .

August 23 . . . I've been working here for almost four weeks, and so far my arms are doing pretty well. I would say I spend less than half my time at the computer, and it's usually never in one long stretch.

Yesterday my boss took me out to lunch. That was quite interesting. She told me everyone was very pleased with my work. Gave me a couple of pointers about things where I could improve.

She was so nice that, without intending to, I found myself confiding in her that I was gay. As soon as I did, I could have bitten my tongue off, but she just laughed and said, "I already had that figured out." Then she told me that she is lesbian and is quite active in a gay-rights group. . . .

Chapter 15

Bittersweet Wedding

Slipping her hand into the crook of Alex's arm, Kate smiled up at him as he escorted her down the aisle of the chapel, crowded with friends and relatives.

Kate had promised herself that she would not be weepy on this happy occasion. To keep at bay the flood of nostalgic memories that threatened to undo her resolve, she concentrated on admiring the elegant simplicity of the colonial-style chapel with its high domed ceiling and crystal chandelier. Tall arched windows of leaded glass, framed with ornate ivory moldings, lined the white walls, giving a sense of brightness and light to the room and visually extending it to include the huge shade trees that surrounded the church. At the front of the church, ivy cascaded from white Grecian urns, and a pair of spiral candelabra were twined with deep pink roses and carnations, white spider mums, and more ivy.

Brenden had been nearing thirty when Melissa stepped into his life like a ray of sunshine. What joy Kate and Michael had shared, watching his quiet personality unfold and blossom as he and Melissa fell in love. What satisfaction to see a beloved son find true happiness with a woman who loved God and shared his ideals. Kate quickly checked that thought before it went too far and looked up as Melissa's mother and father were seated at the opposite end of her pew.

The organist changed to a bright and joyous processional as Michael entered from the front and six pairs of brides-maids and groomsmen swept up both side aisles, the women wearing bouffant dresses of sapphire blue taffeta and the men dashing and handsome in black tuxedos, with bow ties and cummerbunds that echoed the color of the women's dresses. Kate smiled in loving pride as first Alex, then Danny, passed her with beautiful women on their arms. Carefully, she refused to acknowledge painful thoughts that hovered at the edge of her mind.

The organ music became more stately and regal. Following the lead of Melissa's mother, the congregation stood and turned toward the rear of the church. Kate caught her breath, and unshed tears shone in her eyes as she saw Brenden and Melissa, looking like a fairytale prince and princess dressed in white, moving slowly up the opposite aisle. They were preceded by the Bible boy, dressed like a miniature groomsman, and Sara, the flower girl, wearing a dainty white dress Kate had made. Kate flashed a smile at Stephanie, who was in the pew behind her with Amy and Samantha, also wearing pretty dresses lovingly made by their grandmother.

When the bride and groom reached the front of the chapel, the music ended, and heads were bowed as Michael prayed. Then, with a rustle, the congregation was seated, and Michael began his homily.

"Melissa and Brenden, we have come, as your family and friends, to be with you on this special day; to share in your joy; to celebrate with you; and to ask God's blessing as you become a new family in the larger family of God."

As she listened to the beautiful words, Kate's heart overflowed with joy over her son's happiness. And in that unguarded moment, thoughts of another son, thoughts she had studiously avoided all afternoon, suddenly overwhelmed her.

Blinking back tears, Kate fumbled in her handbag for a handkerchief as she remembered another wedding she had once dreamed of. Her gaze shifted from Brenden and Melissa to Danny, standing so straight and handsome in his black tuxedo, and for a moment she felt the weight of unutterable sadness.

A pensive look shadowed Danny's face. Brenden's wedding was a bittersweet occasion for him, he later told his mother. He was glad for his brother. He knew Brenden had waited a long time for the happiness Melissa had brought him. And he was glad to be included and to have an important role in this family occasion. But he could not help comparing his situation with Brenden's as he listened to his father's voice.

"Brenden and Melissa, marriage is a gift to you from God. In the unity of marriage, it is His plan that you will enjoy, together, a wholeness and completeness that you could not experience alone. Your personalities, blended in marriage, will more fully reflect God's divine character."

How Danny yearned for his relationship with Steve to be approved of and accepted by his parents and family, for them to feel joy and happiness for him such as they so freely expressed over Brenden's wedding, for the blessing of the church, the recognition of society. But he knew it would never be. He fought back feelings of hurt and bitterness.

"And so, Melissa and Brenden, it is your love for each other that has brought all of us here for this joyful occasion, your wedding day. As your parents, family, and friends, we wish you every happiness and joy as you begin your life together. May love and laughter crown your home. May God shower His richest blessings on you. And may your love grow deeper and stronger with every passing day."

Michael introduced the new husband and wife, the organist burst into exuberant Mendelssohn, and the happy couple proceeded down the aisle past Kate as the bells in the tower began ringing out the joyful news to the city. As Kate followed the procession out to the vestibule and into the late-afternoon sunshine, the clangor of the bells echoed the exultation of her heart as, for the moment, she completely identified with the celebration of her son's wedding day.

But for Danny, painful longing still clouded the happy occasion. He understood why most of his gay friends refused to attend weddings. It was just too painful!

Chapter 16

Michael

Kate stood in the doorway and squinted at Danny's quilt top spread out on the living-room floor. Squinting gave the effect of seeing it from a distance, so that all the blocks of bright colors, set off by polished black, blended into the abstract design she had first seen in her head.

That's the fascination of quilting, Kate thought, *transforming something from your imagination into something you can see with your eyes. It doesn't always turn out exactly like you thought it would, but it's exciting to watch it taking shape.*

In a way, it's like life, she mused. *Sometimes it's hard to see how all the good and bad things that happen to us fit together to make a design, but God sees how our lives will look when they're finished.*

She went to get her jar of safety pins. After carefully tugging and smoothing the three layers of lining, batting, and quilt top, she began pinning them together at six-inch intervals.

When at last she was finished, she picked up her quilt "sandwich" and carried it over to position it on her large oval hoop. She was ready to begin the second stage—quilting.

Before she started, though, she decided to get some tapes to listen to. Opening the buffet drawer where she kept the ones she listened to most, she pulled out the Brahms *German Requiem* and a Bach violin concerto. Then she saw Danny's cantata. She put that on top of the stack.

She remembered her amazement and delight the first time

she had listened to Danny's composition. She had never before realized that he had such a gift. Putting the cassette into the tape player, she pressed the button, marveling again as she heard the plaintively sweet, pure melody of the first few bars sung by the baritones, then repeated four notes higher by the tenors.

Kate pulled her rocking chair up close to the quilt hoop. She unwound a length of gold thread, pushed it through the eye of her needle, and began taking tiny stitches, following the quilting lines she had marked. Next to seeing the design take shape, this was the part of quilting she loved most. The soothing repetition seemed to release tension and set her mind free to explore in many directions.

With Danny's music as a background to her thoughts, Kate reflected on the growth and changes the last five years had brought to her life.

It was pain that had forced her to surrender Danny to God. She thought of the many times her fears and worries had driven her to the brink of despair. At last, she would realize that there was nothing she could do, and in her extremity she would turn Danny over to God. But sooner or later, she would discover that she had picked up her burden again. It seemed that only through pain could she hear God whisper, "You can trust Danny's future with Me."

Pain had been the catalyst that had changed her preoccupation with daily plans and activities into a deep soul hunger for God. She had searched her Bible with a desperate need for assurance that God was real after all her expectations and dreams had been shattered.

And God had answered, not by taking away her pain, but by making her aware that He was there with her, in the pain. In those moments when she sensed His presence, she felt more fully alive than she ever had before. She had come to the place where she could truly thank God for this, the greatest sorrow of her life, because it had brought her closer to Him.

Pain had also broken down the walls of pride that made her feel she had to look perfect in the eyes of others. Driven by her desperate need, she had shared her heartache with family and friends and found, to her amazement, that they loved her anyway. She discovered that her growing ability to be vulnerable made it easier for others to open up and share their pain with her.

The music had stopped. Kate stuck her needle into the cloth. Closing her eyes, she ran her fingers lightly over the area she had just quilted, feeling the discipline and character the little hills and valleys gave to the fabric.

She stood up and stretched the kinks out of her neck before starting another tape—her favorite, the *German Requiem*. As always, when she heard the haunting melody played by the strings, rising from the deep throbbing bass notes that opened the first chorus, the music spoke to her of hope in the midst of sorrow.

And good has come from pain, thought Kate as she resumed quilting. Their sorrow over Danny's dilemma had drawn her and Michael closer together. At first, of course, it had driven a wall between them, as Michael had reacted to his pain with denial, insisting that Danny was just going through a phase.

Just how and when he had changed, Kate couldn't say. Perhaps it had started on graduation weekend, when Danny's choice of lifestyle had inescapably confronted him. Maybe it was then that he had begun to face the fact that Danny's problem was not going to disappear.

And perhaps, thought Kate, *his attitude has changed because I've shared things I've learned about homosexuality with him.*

From the beginning, Kate had dealt with her pain by seeking to learn and understand more about homosexuality. She remembered one day when she had gone to the doctor's office for her checkup. It had been a cold, windy day, and the streets were slick with rain. Inside, it was overheated and stuffy, the waiting room crowded with sneezing, sniffling patients and crying children. Kate had found a chair in the corner, pulled out her bag of quilt pieces, and retreated to a quiet mental oasis.

When the nurse came to the door and called a name, the

plump woman in a threadbare green coat, sitting next to Kate, had stood up and laid the magazine she had been reading on her chair. Kate had glanced over at the magazine, a *Newsweek*, then quickly looked back again, her attention arrested by the picture of a baby's face on the cover, headlined with the question "Is This Child Gay?"

Slowly she had laid her quilting down in her lap and reached over to pick up the magazine. Turning to the cover article, she began reading about the debate over nature versus nurture—whether homosexuality is inherited or caused by environmental influences. One of the most interesting features of the article was a sidebar about research done on homosexual men who had died of AIDS. It showed that in homosexual men, the part of the hypothalamus gland that controls sex is small, like that of females, while in heterosexual men, it was considerably larger. While scientists didn't draw any conclusions about inheritance of homosexual tendencies from this data, it was one more piece of evidence that helped Kate to understand that perhaps Danny was different physically, not just mentally.

The nurse had called Kate to see Dr. Zimmerman before she finished reading, so when she left the office she drove to the library, found the same issue of *Newsweek*, and copied the article.

Sitting in her car, with rain beating on the windshield, she finished reading it before driving back to her office. The overall impression she got was that there were nearly as many opinions regarding the cause of homosexuality and what should or could be done about it as there were people interviewed.

For Kate, this article confirmed her conclusion that homosexuality was a very complex condition; many different factors might contribute to it, but only in people who had that tendency to begin with.

After supper that evening, she laid the article on the table in front of Michael. "Honey, I saw this at the doctor's office this afternoon," she said as she picked up their empty soup bowls and carried them to the sink. "It was so interesting I made a copy for you."

Michael had scraped his chair back from the table and stood up. Noncommittally, he picked up the article and carried it into the family room. When Kate looked in a few minutes later, he was reading it.

He never mentioned his reaction to it, but Kate felt sure that under his calm exterior, Michael was going through the same anguish she had already experienced. And although he hadn't been able to talk about it, she sensed he appreciated her attempts to communicate.

Slanting rays of the afternoon sun reached her quilt and brought Kate's mind back to the present, reminding her that the weekend would soon be over. It was time to take a break from quilting. She decided to drive to the nearby park and gardens where she and Michael always loved to walk.

The parking lot was full, even though most of the azaleas and rhododendrons had finished blooming, and Kate had to wait for a car to leave. Wanting more solitude than the popular gardens afforded, she crossed the bridge over the little stream and took a path through the woods. She always felt as if she were entering a dim, cool cathedral when she walked here. Leafy green branches towered above her, and evening bird calls lent an atmosphere of peaceful relaxation.

As she followed the trail around the lake, Kate remembered another educational experience she had shared with Michael.

They had been enjoying a quiet weekend getaway at their friends' condo on the ocean. After a morning of walking the beach and letting the rhythm of crashing waves slow their pulse, they had returned to the condo for lunch.

While Kate put together sandwiches and a salad, Michael had turned on the TV. Switching channels, he stopped at a broadcast of the Senate hearings on lifting the ban on gays in the military. Kate brought their plates in, and they ate as they watched.

Senators were questioning a panel of officers from various branches of the military who opposed lifting the ban. Kate had been amazed at the stereotyped views and the degree of prejudice so blatantly expressed. With obvious difficulty, one panel member, a career army officer, admitted that his son had told him he was gay just before the hearings began. He stated that, as much as he loved his son, he would have to advise him that there was no place for him in the military.

Kate and Michael had finished eating, but neither one made a move to return to the beach. The next panel to come before the committee was composed of those who favored lifting the ban. It included a highly decorated gay air force officer; a lesbian army nurse with a Ph.D., who had been awarded the highest honors before she revealed her orientation; and an ex-marine who had served as a member of an elite squadron before his homosexual orientation became known.

In contrast to the first panel, they spoke with dignity and restraint, sharing something of the struggles they had gone through in coming to terms with their homosexuality, the dedication and love they felt for their country, and the high quality of their military service.

Tears had filled Kate's eyes. At one point, she burst out, "How could anyone not feel sympathy for them?" Michael didn't answer, but when Kate glanced at him, he had a very thoughtful look on his face.

The fourth member of the panel was a navy officer who, during his career as a submarine commander, had several times had a homosexual crew member. He stated that this had never caused any problems, even though a submarine was a very confined area.

Learning more about homosexuality has surely made it easier for Michael to understand and accept Danny, Kate decided as she got back to her car. She thought about all the books she had read on the subject. Two, in particular, that she had shared with him had had an impact.

Once, in her search for someone with whom she could share her pain and questions, Kate had attended a P-FLAG (Parents and Friends of Lesbians and Gays) meeting. She had found a warm, supportive atmosphere, although she could not feel comfortable with their strong pro-gay stance.

After the meeting, she had browsed through their library and checked out a book Neil Miller's *In Search of Gay America* described a journalist's year-long travels around the country to seek out and interview homosexuals and lesbians in every walk of life. The thing that had impressed Kate most about the report was that the vast majority of them seemed to lead very normal, respectable, ordinary lives—from a pair of dairy farmers in Wisconsin to a successful politician in the South to restaurant entrepreneurs in Colorado.

"You hear so much about the sordid, perverted side of homosexuality," Michael had said after he read it, "but I suppose that probably involves only a small minority."

The most helpful book Kate had ever read was *Where Does a Mother Go to Resign?*, written by Barbara Johnson, a Christian mother, who shared the incredible pain and depression she went through after learning of her son's homosexuality and her long, slow journey back to recovery. Kate had identified with much of what she had gone through, but the book meant even more because of the hope it projected.

Possibly because the reaction of the author's husband was almost identical to his, after reading this book, Michael had begun talking more freely to Kate about Danny's homosexuality.

Relaxed and pleasantly tired from her long walk, Kate drove home through the gathering evening. As she watched the setting sun brush the clouds, one by one, with delicate pink, she was still thinking about what a difference it had made in their relationship, now that she and Michael were able to talk freely about Danny and share their feelings. They had both become more mature, more sensitive to other people's heartaches, more able to reach out.

Still, she had been surprised, even shocked, the day Michael had come home and told her about a board meeting he had attended. It was the board of a large church institution.

"We discussed hiring policies," he said. "The president told us that no discrimination will be allowed, whether due to race, gender, age, or handicaps. Then he said, 'There is only one point at which I draw the line. We will never hire a homosexual.' "

Kate had gasped in dismay. That could have been her son they were talking about!

"I didn't say anything then," Michael had told her, "but after the meeting I stayed and talked to him. I told him I didn't think such a policy would be following the example of Jesus. I reminded him that there are many homosexuals who choose not to follow that lifestyle. I don't think I changed his mind, but at least I may have given him something to think about."

Kate had slipped her arms around Michael's neck and kissed him tenderly. "Honey, I'm proud of you," she whispered, with tears in her eyes.

Michael had surprised her again, just a few weeks ago, she remembered. He had been asked to give the sermon in another church, and she had accompanied him. Having heard his sermon before, Kate's attention had wandered momentarily. Suddenly, she had been startled into alertness, every nerve tingling, as she heard him say, "God calls us, His children, to reach out to those in our church, and to those who used to be in our church, who may feel defeated and rejected—to pregnant teenagers, to those enslaved by drugs and alcohol, to homosexuals." She had stared proudly at him through eyes blurred with tears.

Back home, Kate parked under the elm tree and walked up the flagstone path through the lavender dusk of a perfect spring evening. The air was fragrant with the scent of lilacs. As she climbed the steps to the porch, a small, furry body rubbed against her ankles. She picked up the tidy little black cat and cuddled her under her chin.

Kate felt at peace with her world as she sat down in the porch rocker to enjoy the end of the day. Her happiness stemmed not only from the new rapport she and Michael enjoyed, but from the knowledge that Michael and Danny were reaching out for a closer relationship too.

Last Christmas, for instance. Instead of a present, Danny had written Michael a special letter. Michael had shared it with Kate. She recalled an excerpt from it:

> I've been wanting to talk to you, Dad, but it's hard to have this kind of conversation over the phone. I've wanted to tell you how it made me feel, the last time you were here, when you told me just before you left that you were proud of me. It felt good, Dad—so good. I felt warm all over and even wanted to cry. The reason I didn't say anything at the time is that I was so taken by surprise that I didn't know how to react. But now that I have processed it, I want to thank you. Dad, I'm thankful that you are my father.

Kate had read Michael's answering letter too. It began:

> Danny, first of all, I want you to know that no dad could love his son more than I do you. I have cried in my heart many times because of the frustration, anguish, and anger you have experienced because of this handicap you were apparently born with. I am sure that at times you have felt there was nowhere to turn and that even God had forsaken you! But there is a spiritual battle being fought in this world, and the devil is out to destroy humanity any way he can. Someday, God's patient love will bring this war to an end, but in the meantime, we are all being tested and tried.

Yes, Kate thought, as she put Beethoven down and went into the house, *God has brought something good out of this, and I know I can trust Him with Danny's future.*

Chapter 17

Danny's Decision

It was a crisp, sunny autumn Sunday. Under a brilliant blue sky, the dogwoods were already a rich maroon, and here and there, other trees sported a branch of scarlet or gold as they began to change into their vivid fall garb.

With an exhilarating sense of well-being, Kate hummed along with the Strauss waltz on the radio as she drove away from the nursery. Back home, she parked her car under the elm tree. She opened the trunk and carefully lifted out three round orange pumpkins of graduated size and carried them to the porch. Then she returned to get several big pots of bronze and white chrysanthemums and a bunch of Indian corn. When she had them arranged to her satisfaction, she stepped back to admire her fall display.

It was warm in the sun, and Kate needed a drink. The phone was ringing as she opened the front door, and she hurried to answer it.

"Hi, Mom!"

"Oh, hi, Danny!" Kate said animatedly. "What have you been doing today?"

For a while, they caught up on important and not-so-important news in each other's lives. But after a slight pause in the conversation, Danny's voice became more serious as he said, "I think maybe this is the time for me to tell you something, Mom. Two things, actually. One thing, I think—no, I'm sure—will make you deliriously happy. The other thing, I hope you will be happy about."

"Well, you've certainly gotten my curiosity aroused," Kate chuckled, although Danny's words made her brace herself.

"Let's see," Danny began. "Maybe I need to lead up to this. I think I told you once that one of my college teachers, Pat Walker, had 'blessed' me with what she called 'the gift of doubt.' It was a gift that was both good and bad. Going way back to the year I stayed home and went to college back there, I had questions about God and religion that needed answers.

"I remember that back then, I talked to Jesus one time and told Him that I was beginning a spiritual quest. I told Him that I knew I might come to the place where I would no longer believe in Him, but I said that while I still did believe, I wanted to ask Him to stay with me on my journey and bring me through to a stronger faith."

Kate listened quietly as Danny talked, but her heart thrilled with anticipation.

"It hasn't been an easy journey, Mom. You have had glimpses of it from time to time. I did get to the place where I didn't believe in God anymore. I didn't believe in anything. It was terrible. I got to where I couldn't even articulate the questions I had; I didn't know what they were anymore. It was like my mind was in a fog. But God didn't leave me, Mom. I feel like He honored my integrity, because through it all I was searching for the truth.

"And here's the part that I know is going to make you very happy. About six weeks or so ago, I made a decision. A number of different things entered into it, but at any rate, I have decided I want to try celibacy. I've bought a futon, and that's where I sleep now—by myself."

A deep feeling of joy and gratitude filled Kate, but, at the same time, it was tempered by a premonition of what was still to come.

"It's really interesting. I didn't know how Steve would take it, but he was ready for it too. It turned out to be a relief for both of us. I haven't made a final decision, and I've slipped up a few times, but so far I'm really happy about it.

"And, Mom, here's the other part I *hope* you'll be happy about. When I started attending St. Andrew's, it was just because of Steve and the choir. But right away, I felt a sense of belonging and being needed. I began to hear God talking to me again. Mom, God has given me back the faith of my childhood—something I thought was gone forever!

"There just isn't a place for me in our church anymore. So, Mom . . . , I have decided to take studies, and I am thinking seriously about joining St. Andrew's. . . . I wanted to let you know that's where I'm headed right now."

Kate drew a deep breath. "Well, you're right, buddy. I did have a feeling this was coming. Oh, Danny, I know God has been leading you. And as long as you keep praying for His guidance, I'm very, very happy. I certainly don't think that only members of our church are going to be saved.

"I'm willing to leave your spiritual future in God's hands, Danny. I just pray that you will keep an open mind and ask God to help you not to be deceived. You know, I believe Satan is very real, and, as the Bible says, he is like a roaring lion, seeking someone to devour."

"I believe that too, Mom," Danny concurred.

"Well, buddy, I want you to know that I believe what you've told me is an answer to prayer, both yours and ours. And I'll keep on praying that God will continue to show you what He wants you to do with your life."

"Mom, I have felt your prayers following me through this wilderness. I'm glad you understand and are happy. I feel so much happier and more at peace now than I used to."

After she hung up, Kate sat quietly, processing feelings of joy and gratitude, as well as feelings of disappointment that Danny had regained his faith through another church.

Oh, Father, she prayed, *that's an unworthy thought. I know that all heaven is rejoicing because a lost sheep has been found! And I am rejoicing too, Father! On that black day when I first learned about Danny's homosexuality, I could never have imagined that I would someday feel joy like this.*

Continued evidence of the change in Danny's life brought new hope to Kate and Michael. A letter from him arrived in their mailbox a month or so after his phone call. He wrote:

I wish I could be there to talk with you about what has happened to me. Three things are coinciding in my spiritual life at this time, and two of them, I'm sure, you're very glad of. First, I've become obedient to our Lord again. This can only have made you glad. Second, because of this, I am embracing celibacy. Again, shouts of joy and thanksgiving. But third, I am joining another church.

It's hard to discuss something that we disagree about and still be supportive of each other. I wish I could share with you the aspects of this faith that excite me, the discovered and rediscovered joys. This is the greatest and most exciting thing in my life right now, and I want you to share in my joy.

God has had mercy on me, a sinner. He has heard my prayer and yours and the prayers of many others and has fixed in my heart lively sentiments of faith, hope, charity, true contrition for my sins, and a firm purpose of amendment.

I will be joining St. Andrew's, God willing, before Christmas. I would like to have your blessing.

As happy as this made them, it was also very difficult for Kate and Michael. That they made an effort to reach out and share this experience with Danny was a measure of their new maturity and understanding. Michael answered Danny:

Your letter was so much appreciated. It helped me know that you understand the promise of Jesus when He said, 'I will never leave you, nor forsake you.' I, too, have come to cherish that text during these last few years. Jesus is such a close friend. I love Him dearly, and I know you do too.

Danny, as I have learned to understand your situation, I have come to greatly admire you. First, because you have continued to love people even when they did not understand you. That's what Jesus did. Second, because you have had the courage to become celibate. Only your love for Jesus and your willingness to obey Him could have brought this about.

Danny, Mom and I have one great wish for all of our children, and that is to meet them in heaven someday. Our prayers are with you every day. God is so good to answer our prayers in your behalf.

A few weeks later, they received a devotional book that Danny wanted to share with them, and accompanying it was the score of a new anthem he had written on the text, "If anyone would come after me, he must deny himself and take up his cross and follow me."

Tears filled Kate's eyes as she thought of the meaning of this verse in Danny's life. Anxious to hear the music, she made copies and persuaded the choir director to have the choir read through it at rehearsal the following week.

She also read the book Danny had sent and shared with him some insights she had gained from it.

"I'm glad you liked it, Mom," Danny said. "I wasn't sure if you'd be willing to read it. I'm really glad we can still communicate about something that's so important to both of us."

As shorter days and frosty nights heralded the approach of winter, Kate spent every spare moment working on Danny's quilt. She wanted to have it finished in time for Christmas.

It was going to be a Christmas to remember! The children were all coming home this year! Danny, Brenden and Melissa, and Alex and Stephanie, with Amy, Sara, and Samantha.

Finally, the last stitch was taken. Kate hung the quilt over the banister so she could admire the fine gold quilting, the diagonal lines giving each bright triangle a jewel-like facet. Then she folded it carefully, wrapped it in tissue paper, and put it in a large coat box.

Now she could turn her attention to Christmas baking and decorating. There were pecan pies and fancy braided Christmas breads, Danny's favorite French rolls, and nut-encrusted thumbprint cookies, their indentations filled with sparkling red and green jelly, to make. The house smelled heavenly.

A cluster of pine cones, topped with a big red bow, decked the front door. The staircase banister was entwined with a pine garland and tiny white Christmas lights. Tall red candles in brass candlesticks stood among the pine boughs on the mantle, and a basket of red and pink poinsettias decorated the hearth. In the center of the dining table stood a crystal bowl holding a fat red candle nestled in a bed of greenery. A basket of gold-tipped pine cones, with a red bow on the handle, adorned the coffee table.

To complete the house's festive air, Michael brought home a beautiful eight-foot-tall Christmas tree and set it up in the corner of the family room. Together, he and Kate wound strings of tiny white lights among the branches and hung most of the ornaments, saving out a few of the older ones for the children and grandchildren to hang when they arrived.

"Oh, honey, look!" Kate exclaimed delightedly. Big snowflakes were gently hitting the windshield as she and Michael drove to the airport on the afternoon of Christmas Eve to pick up their California kids. "The perfect touch!" she said softly.

Dusk was falling, and it was snowing harder by the time their merry group had stowed all the luggage in the trunk and packed themselves into the car for the ride home. Brenden and Melissa arrived from Virginia in time for supper.

Later, they gathered around the tree to open presents. The big box for Danny was on the bottom of the heap. All eyes were on him as he began to unwrap it.

"Bet I know what this is," he said, giving Kate a loving grin.

"Hurry up, Uncle Danny!" Sara shouted impatiently.

Slowly, Danny opened the box, pushed back the tissue paper, and lifted out the quilt. As it spilled over his lap and fell in folds to the floor, a thousand memories of all the tears that had been shed and prayers that had ascended flashed through Kate's mind. A long look passed between her and Danny, and then she stood up and went to him.

"It's beautiful, Mom," he said as they hugged each other.

Kate kissed him on the top of his head. "As beautiful as your life," she whispered softly.